CATE TIERNAN

WICCA

ORIGINS

The eleventh book in the series

PUFFIN BOOKS

PUFFIN BOOKS

Published by the Penguin Group
Penguin Books Ltd, 80 Strand, London WC2R 0RL, England
Penguin Putnam Inc., 375 Hudson Street, New York, New York 10014, USA
Penguin Books Australia Ltd, 250 Camberwell Road, Camberwell, Victoria 3124, Australia
Penguin Books Canada Ltd, 10 Alcorn Avenue, Toronto, Ontario, Canada M4V 3B2
Penguin Books India (P) Ltd, 11 Community Centre, Panchsheel Park, New Delhi – 110 017, India
Penguin Books (NZ) Ltd, Cnr Rosedale and Airborne Roads, Albany, Auckland, New Zealand
Penguin Books (South Africa) (Pty) Ltd, 24 Sturdee Avenue, Rosebank 2196, South Africa

Penguin Books Ltd, Registered Offices: 80 Strand, London WC2R 0RL, England

www.penguin.com

First published in the USA in Puffin Books, a division of Penguin Putnam Books for Young Readers,
2002
Published in Great Britain in Puffin Books 2003

Printed in England by Clays Ltd, St Ives plc

British Library Cataloguing in Publication Data
A CIP catalogue record for this book is available from the British Library

ISBN 0–141–31552–0

With thanks to Silver,
And with love for my children of
the Barley and Snow Moons

Prologue

"Hey, Morgan!"

Afternoon sunlight bounced off the cars in the high school parking lot as I turned to face my best friend, Bree Warren. I knew that she was eager to catch up with me—I'd been kind of cranky and out of sorts all week—but at the moment I was in a huge hurry. I leaned against the driver's side of my huge '71 Chrysler Valiant, which I'd nicknamed "Das Boot."

"What's up, Bree?"

Bree ran up and stopped a few feet away from me, gasping for breath. "I just wanted to sort of check in, see how you were doing today."

I nodded. "Well, I heard from Hunter last night. I'm supposed to go to his house now."

Her eyes widened in comprehension. "*Oh*. So Hunter's back."

"Apparently so." Hunter Niall, my boyfriend of two months—was it possible it had only been that long? I couldn't imagine life without him. I loved him with all my heart and soul and was fairly certain that he was my mùirn beatha dàn, my soul mate.

He had left a little over two weeks ago to find his parents.

"Are you nervous?" Bree looked at me sympathetically .

"A little." I sighed. All the time Hunter had been gone, we'd had only one conversation. Worried, I had scried for him and found him with another woman. Not kissing or anything romantic—thank the Goddess for that—but locked in a passionate conversation. I wasn't sure what to make of the whole thing. I was afraid to think too hard about it.

"I'm sure it'll be okay," she said confidently. "Hunter loves you, Morgan. You can see it in his eyes when he looks at you. You have nothing to worry about."

I looked up at Bree, feeling a little comforted. "Thanks. I just love him so much. . . . Well, you know how I feel."

She nodded. "I don't want to keep you, then." She smoothed down a lock of shiny dark hair and gave me a concerned frown. "Listen, I hope everything's okay. I know you've been worried. Let me know if you need to talk, all right?"

"All right." I smiled. It seemed like Bree had gotten even more beautiful, more caring, more empathetic since she had fallen in love with my other best friend, Robbie Gurevitch. Not that she'd been totally selfish before—she just seemed warmer now, more open.

"See you tomorrow."

"Bye."

Bree headed back toward the school and Robbie, and I climbed into Das Boot and swung out of the parking lot. It was mid-March, and the sidewalks were still covered with glistening, melting snow. I tried to calm my nerves as I drove toward Hunter's rented house on the other side of town. But the truth was, I was very afraid. Afraid of what Hunter would tell me. Afraid that I wouldn't want to hear it.

After I arrived, I sat in Hunter's driveway for a few minutes with the car running, trying to collect my thoughts. On the one hand, this was Hunter. Hunter, who I loved and had missed terribly—I couldn't wait to see him. But on the other hand, what if he had found something new and wonderful in Canada? What if that was why he hadn't called me? What if he had been afraid to tell me something hurtful over the phone?

Sighing, I pulled the key from the ignition and smoothed my worn cords. I ran a quick hand through my long brown hair and decided that taming it was a lost cause. Taking a deep breath, I climbed out of Das Boot and headed for the door. I reached out my hand to ring the doorbell, but before I could get there, the door opened.

"Morgan."

"Hunter." As soon as I saw Hunter's face—serious, loving—my fears and anger faded away. I wrapped my arms around him, buried my face in the crook of his neck, and breathed in his warm, familiar scent.

"I missed you," I murmured into his collar. "I was so worried."

"I know, love." I could feel Hunter's hand rubbing my back, his other hand reaching up to stroke my hair. "I missed you, too. I wanted you there with me every moment."

"*Every* moment?" I asked, unable to prevent myself from picturing him arguing with the woman from my vision.

"Every moment." Hunter leaned back and looked at me, then turned and gestured to his living room. "Sit down for a moment and let me get you some tea. There's lots to talk about."

I nodded, pulling off my coat and looking around. "Where's your father?" Our phone conversation the night before had been very brief, largely due to the fact that it was after midnight and my mother was standing beside me in the hallway with steam coming out of her ears because he'd called so late. All I had learned from Hunter was that he had found his dad, who was in poor health, and that he had convinced him to come back with him to Widow's Vale. His mother, unfortunately, had died three months earlier, around Yule. Hunter hadn't said as much, but I could sense his frustration at not finding her in time and his grief over losing the mother he'd had so little time with.

"He's asleep," Hunter called, heading for the kitchen. "He's been sleeping almost nonstop since we left his cottage. I'm hoping that all the rest will be good for him. He certainly needs it."

I settled on the sofa, and after a few minutes Hunter joined me, holding two cups of chamomile tea. "For you," he said, handing a cup to me and sitting down. "I think we could both use some soothing after the past couple of weeks."

I sipped my tea, closed my eyes, and tried to let all of my fears, all of my insecurities and anger run out of me. "Hunter," I said finally, feeling more calm, "tell me what happened in Canada."

Hunter's jaw tightened almost imperceptibly, and I saw a darkness pass over his eyes. "It was . . . difficult." He paused and sipped his tea. "I feel like I've been tested in ways I never could have predicted or imagined. My mum is dead." He looked at me briefly, and I nodded slowly. "She and my da had been on the run from the dark wave for all those years—eleven years." He sighed. "It was Selene, you know. Selene Belltower sent the dark wave after them because she couldn't forgive my da for leaving her and Cal."

I gasped. Selene Belltower and her son, Cal, had first introduced me to the world of Wicca. It was Cal who told me I was a blood witch. I'd then realized that I was adopted, that I was the biological daughter of Maeve Riordan and Ciaran MacEwan—two very powerful, and very different, witches. I had thought that Cal was my true love, my mùirn beatha dàn, but it turned out that he was a pawn of his mother, who wanted to harness my power for her own dark uses. And I'd learned that before Hunter was born, his father had loved and married Selene, making Cal Hunter's half brother. Both Cal and Selene were dead now—Selene had died trying to steal my power, and in the end Cal had died trying to save me.

"It was Selene?" I asked finally, and Hunter nodded.

"My mum scried for the dark wave in Mexico, and she got too close. She was never the same after that, and she died last December. After that my da moved to a tiny village in French Canada. He was living in filth, like a madman. I found out he was acting as a sort of medicine man to the local population, selling his services as a witch, which was bad enough. But I soon realized that he was also doing something much worse—he was contacting the villagers' dead loved ones through a bith dearc and receiving payment for it."

I looked at Hunter in disbelief. "Contacting the dead? I didn't think that was possible."

Hunter nodded again. "It is. A bith dearc is an opening into the shadow world where spirits reside after they die. It doesn't naturally occur very often, and it's very rarely used by 'good' witches—only when it's imperative to get information. My father began using the bith dearc to try and contact my mother. He's utterly lost without her." Hunter's mouth twisted into a strange expression—he looked angry, sad, and understanding of his father's devotion all at the same time.

"Wow," I said softly. "How horrible for your dad. How horrible for *you*." I touched his arm, and he looked up at me gratefully.

"Anyway," he continued, "while I was there, he succeeded in contacting my mum. So I got to say good-bye to her, which was—priceless. But a bith dearc saps a living witch's strength, and my da was fading every day. I had to get him away from that village before he killed himself. The council gave me an assignment in a town three hours away, and I took him with me. While we were there, he agreed to come here to live with me for a while." Hunter turned to me and smiled and shrugged, as if to say, "The end."

"That's not everything, though," I challenged. "There was a woman. I saw you with her. I know you felt me scrying for you."

Hunter's smile faded, and he nodded. "Justine," he said quietly. "Justine Courceau. She was my assignment from the council."

Hunter was a Seeker for the International Council of Witches, which meant that he investigated witches suspected of using dark magick. "What was she doing?" I asked.

Hunter sighed. "She's a kind of—rogue. She's the only witch in her small town, and she believes that knowledge is pure—any knowledge. She was collecting true names . . . of people." My eyes went wide. That was a major Wiccan no-no. "I was sent there to stop her and destroy her list."

"Did you?" I asked, remembering the emotion on Hunter's face when I had scried for him.

"Yes." Hunter frowned, and his voice grew softer. "Justine was very passionate about what she believed in. When you saw us, we were arguing about whether the list was inherently bad. I was under a lot of stress, and she was very—persistent."

I stared at him, dreading his next words.

"I kissed her," Hunter continued, and my heart plunged. "I

knew as soon as I did it that it was a mistake. I was lonely and . . . sad. I missed you. I wanted you." Hunter groaned softly. I turned away. I felt like I had been kicked in the stomach. I couldn't look at him right now.

"How does kissing another woman . . . mean that you want to spend time with *me*?" I stared at the wall. I couldn't imagine wanting to kiss anyone else, anyone but Hunter, for any reason. I struggled to get it all to make sense, but I just couldn't.

I could hear Hunter's sigh. "I don't know, Morgan, and I'm sorry. So sorry. If there was some way that I could undo it, I would."

I shook my head. "But you can't."

"I know." I felt Hunter's fingers touch my back, but I scooted away. "Morgan, I don't know what to say, how to explain it all to you. I love you very much. You're my mùirn beatha dàn, and I know that."

I let out a ragged breath, like I was about to cry. Dammit—no! I took a deep lungful of air, not wanting to fall apart in front of Hunter. I wanted to hear what he had to say about this. I wanted to act like an adult.

Hunter went on. "The whole drive home, you were all I could think about. If you want to know why in that moment I kissed Justine, I can scarcely figure it out myself. It happened quickly. I felt like everything in my life was going the wrong way. My job with the council, my father—"

"—and me," I finished for him. "Because I scried for you. Without asking. And before you left—" My voice caught again. Before Hunter left, we had been planning to make love. But at the last minute Hunter had backed out. He'd said he didn't want to love me and leave me—he wanted to be there for me, my first time, on the morning after. I had felt ridiculous then, and I felt even more so now.

Hunter put his hand on my shoulder, and this time I was too busy trying not to cry to pull away. "Morgan, this has nothing to do with what happened before I left. I love you, and of course I want to make love with you—it just wasn't the right time. You know that. I was startled when you scried for me, and every-thing else was going wrong. I suppose I was angry. I was wrong, and I'm sorry. Justine means nothing to me. It's you I love."

Sniffling, I tried to calm myself down. I reached for my tea and took a sip, then sighed and slowly turned my body to face Hunter. "I know you do," I whispered. "It just . . . hurts. And I still don't understand."

Hunter frowned, leaning forward to brush my hair out of my eyes. "Maybe I can't make you understand," he said softly. "I can only say again that I love you, and I'm so sorry for hurting you."

I looked up into Hunter's eyes—they were warm, filled with concern and love. But I still hurt. "Maybe," I said softly. "I can't say I forgive you yet. You'll have to give me some time."

Hunter nodded, and I could see sadness welling up in his eyes. "Morgan, I can't say I'm sorry enough."

I looked down at my tea, cradling the cup in my hands. I didn't say anything. I didn't know what to say anymore.

Hunter sat back in the sofa. "Morgan, there's more news—if you want to hear it."

I turned the teacup in my hand, feeling utterly overwhelmed. "What next?" I asked sarcastically. I was dreading his next revela-tion. Everything up to this point had been awful.

"First," he said after a moment, "the council. Morgan, the council had been in contact with my parents months ago—

back when my mother was sick, before she died. They knew where my parents were and didn't tell me."

I turned to look at him. "What? How do you know? Are you sure?"

Hunter nodded. "My da told me. He thought I already knew. My mentor, Kennet—he sent a healer for my mum back in December."

I frowned. "So—"

"So they betrayed me. They probably wanted me here, to protect you. And I don't regret that—truly, I don't regret that at all. But they didn't give me the choice. They let me believe that my parents were still missing."

I stared at him, at the hurt in his face. I could see how this would affect him. He had missed seeing his mother alive because he'd had to stay here and protect *me*. Hunter had placed all of his trust in the council since he had become their youngest Seeker a year ago, and this was how they treated him. "What are you going to do?"

Hunter shook his head. "I don't know."

I slowly put my cup down. "Was there something else?" I asked shortly, dreading the answer.

Hunter nodded, looking stung. I knew he wanted forgiveness, but I wasn't ready to give him that. "Stay here for a moment," he said as he slid off the couch and went upstairs to his bedroom. In a few seconds he thumped back down the stairs, holding an ancient-looking book under his arm.

"What's that?"

Hunter came closer and held it out to me. "This is very interesting. It's a record of sorts. My father found it in Justine's library."

I shuddered at hearing her name again, but I composed myself and took the book from him carefully, so that I didn't have to touch his hands. I ran my hands over the cover, which was made of torn and faded leather. Opening it, I could see that the pages were handwritten. "A Book of Shadows?"

"Not a Book of Shadows, exactly." Hunter flipped the pages back to the beginning, where a handwritten title page read, *A Book of Spelles and Memories, by Rose MacEwan.* "It's more like a memoir."

"Rose MacEwan," I whispered. "Do you think . . . ?"

Hunter nodded gravely. "She lived in Scotland during the Burning Times. It's very likely that she was an ancestor of yours. This book could be invaluable for what it can tell us about the dark wave spell and how it came into being. My da's read most of it, but I haven't looked at it at all." He closed the cover of the book and looked up at me hopefully. "Would you like to read it with me, Morgan?"

I looked into Hunter's clear green eyes. I could see his love for me, pure and unbending, along with the pain he'd suffered and his hope for the future. My heart still ached with the knowledge of what he'd done, but I hoped that we'd be okay . . . eventually. I turned my attention to the book. When I ran my hand again over the worn embossed cover, I felt a rush of energy. My ancestor. I knew it.

"Yes," I said finally. "Let's read it."

1.

Scotland, April 1680

The rose stone.

It glimmered brightly in my palm, catching the few rays of light allowed in by the drab portals of the church. The reverend mumbled on, glorifying the Christian God. My thoughts were far from the church altar as I considered the spell I would cast over this precious gem.

Beside me, my mother lifted her head from pretending to pray. I closed my fist suddenly, not wanting her to see the stone that I'd borrowed from her cupboard of magickal things. The crystal, with its soft, pink hue, was known to evoke peaceful, loving feelings. It was a wonder to me that I shared the same name as the stone—Rose—yet I had never come close to falling in love. Ma raised her brows, chastising me without words, and I dropped the stone back into my pocket and clasped my hands the way the Presbyterians did.

Would Ma mind that I had borrowed the stone for Kyra? I wondered. Ever since my initiation my mother had encouraged me to work on my own magick, practice my own spells and rituals. But somehow I didn't think she would appreciate that one of my first attempts would be to cast a love spell for my best friend. My mother had warned me against using spells that tamper with a person's free will, but a love spell was for the good, I thought. Besides, Falkner had been oblivious to Kyra for so long, and I knew she was getting desperate.

A few rows ahead Kyra turned to me, her mouth twitching slightly before she turned back to the front of the church. I knew what she was thinking. That church was tedious. Nothing like our beautiful circles in the woods, gatherings lit by candles, sometimes festooned by ribbons, blessed with the magickal presence of the Goddess. Not that I had any quarrel with the Christian God. Time and again Ma had reminded me that they were all the same—God or Goddess, it was one force we worshipped, albeit different forms. The problem was the ministers, who could not open their minds to accept our homage and devotion to the Goddess. Consequently the king's men and the Christians were ever crossing over the countryside in a mad witch-hunt that brought about dire results.

Makeshift trials. Hangings. Witches burned at the stake.

And so every week my mother and I knelt in this church, our heads bowed, our hands folded. We pretended to practice Presbyterianism so that we might avoid the fate suffered by other members of the Seven Clans who had been persecuted for practicing magick, for worshiping the Goddess. The puritanical wave that had been moving through Scotland had claimed many a life. The toll across the land was frightening, with tales of so many witches persecuted, most of them women.

Just last year a woman from our own coven, a gentle wisp of a lass named Fionnula, had been found killing a peahen with a bolline marked with runes. Those of us who knew her understood that the hen was not intended as an offering to the Goddess but as a very necessary meal. Still, the townspeople could not see beyond the fact of the strange markings on the small knife she used to kill the bird. Fionnula had been charged with sacrifice and worshiping the devil.

I lifted my eyes to the altar, staring at the robed back of the murmuring reverend who had been so instrumental in Fionnula's fate. At her trial Reverend Winthrop had testified that the young woman missed his sermon every week, defying the Christian God. He had called her a vassal of Satan.

I clenched my hands, recalling the horrified look in Fionnula's eyes as she was sentenced to death. Christians had come from nearby villages to witness the trial—a ghastly spectacle in these parts—and although every Wodebayne had wanted to save her, no one spoke in her defense. 'Twas far too dangerous.

The following day she was hanged as a witch.

Sometimes when I catch suspicious gestures of the townspeople—a curious stare or a whispered comment—I can't help but recall the fear in Fionnula's dark eyes. Her execution brought a new veil of secrecy to our circles. More rules passed down by my mother, who was sometimes a bit overbearing in her role as high priestess. Ma wanted me to see less of my friend Meara, a kind girl who loved to laugh but was born into a staid Presbyterian family. Everyone in the coven had been warned to take great care in all their associations, whether it be trading baked goods for mutton or simply washing garments in the brook. No one outside our all-Wodebayne coven was to be trusted.

Tools were to be well hidden and guarded by spells that made them unnoticeable. Skyclad circles were no longer safe, and when we gathered for an Esbat or a Sabbat circle, coveners went into the woods in small groups of two. We were so afraid of being caught that we tried not to be seen gathering together at market or in the village—nothing beyond a cordial greeting. And now every member of the coven attended church every Sunday.

We were prisoners in our own village. By night we practiced our craft in secret. By day we played at being just like the rest of the townspeople.

The injustice of it fired up a fury within me. That my mother—Síle, high priestess of our coven—should have to kneel amidst their wooden pews . . . It was a travesty, to be sure. Just one of the heavy burdens upon my shoulders, making me feel like a trapped animal in a dark sack that was closing in around me. There were so many rules governing my world. I had to hide the fact that I was a blood witch from the townfolk. I had to avoid contact with other clans, whose members considered themselves our rivals although we were all witches and worshiped the same Goddess. (This was a tedious war, I felt, but I had been told the rivalry among the Seven Clans had worn on through many generations.) I had to make entries into my Book of Shadows, gather and dry herbs, learn to make healing tonics and candles, bless and inscribe my own tools. . . .

Aye, the life of Rose MacEwan was filled with constraints. Was it any wonder that I felt suffocated by them?

When I thought of what would make me happy, the answer was not forthcoming. I wasn't quite sure of my own heart's desire; however, I knew that my destiny was not to spend the rest of my life concocting spells and practicing witchcraft secretly in this remote, provincial village.

At last the prayers ended and townsfolk began to file out of the church. I waded into the aisle, hoping to catch Kyra before her parents whisked her back to their cottage. Kyra was my lifelong friend, a member of my clan and coven, though she was not as adept at casting spells as I was said to be.

Wouldn't she be surprised to see what I'd brought for her? I reached into the pocket of my skirts and closed my hand around the small gem. My fingertips felt warmed by the stone. I planned to give it to Kyra to help her attract Falkner Radburn, a boy from our own Wodebayne coven. Falkner was all Kyra had spoken of since the children jumped the broomstick at Samhain. All winter long I had heard of Falkner's strength and Falkner's eyes. Falkner this and Falkner that. Bad enough that poor Kyra was captivated by him, but to make matters worse, Falkner was unaware of her love.

I had agreed to help my friend, though I didn't really understand why she favored him. Then again, I had never known any attraction like that. In my eyes boys were silly galloping creatures, and men had nothing to do with me. They seemed to me like the wolves who roamed at night, pouncing on their prey without warning. I was a Wodebayne of seventeen years, initiated into the ways of the Goddess at fourteen, and as most girls my age were already betrothed or wed, I had come to the conclusion that I would never meet a man who caught my fancy. Since it hadn't happened as yet, I felt that the Goddess didn't intend it to be.

Outside the church, Ma greeted the Presbyterian villagers cordially. I kept my head bowed, not wanting to meet their eyes or see the cruel faces that had so quickly sentenced Fionnula to death. Some time had passed since her trial, yet I could not forgive these people for their crime. I would never forgive them.

"Good day to you, Rose," said a familiar voice.

I turned to see Meara, her freckled face wrought with shadows. "Meara, I didn't see you inside."

"Da and I were late getting in. Ma was up all night with the pains, but she's back resting again. Da said we should come to church and pray to Christ Jesus for her recovery."

Meara's mother had not truly recovered from the birth of her sixth child a few months earlier, and as the oldest daughter, the burden of taking over her ma's responsibilities fell on Meara's shoulders. I felt sorry for her, having to tidy up the cottage, mind the young bairns, and cook enough porridge for the whole brood of them.

"Who's caring for the children, then?" I asked her.

"Ma's sister, Linette, has come from the south to help for a while." Her eyes were hollow, and I wasn't sure if it was simply tiredness or fear over what might happen to her mother. Ma had visited Meara's mother once, hoping to help. She told me they'd talked awhile and she had tried to raise the woman's spirits, but 'twas all Ma could do. She didn't dare pass on healing herbs or place her hands on the ailing woman's worn belly to perform a spell. And that was the shame of it; Ma had the power to perhaps cure Meara's mother, but since that very act could get Ma hanged as a witch, it would not be done.

"I haven't seen you down by the brook lately," Meara told me. "Do you not draw water for washing?"

"Ma sends me later now," I said awkwardly. "She says the

morning chill is too much." It was a lie, and I hated telling it to Meara, who had always been a good friend. But the truth was, Ma had told me to find a different place to draw water so that I wouldn't meet Meara every morning. "It's too dangerous, the two of you talking with such ease," Ma had told me. "One of these days you're liable to slip and speak the Goddess's name or mention the coming Esbat, and that sort of breach I cannot allow."

Meara's father summoned her from the edge of the crowd.

"I'd better go," Meara said reluctantly, "Godspeed."

I nodded, wondering what would happen to my friend if her ma passed. Already Meara was acting as mother to the large family. My own father had died when I was but five years of age, and though I often wished for the protection a father could offer, I remembered so little of him. Losing a mother had to be worse.

"Tell your ma . . ." I wanted to espouse an herbal tea that would help her mother feel better, but I knew it was too dangerous. I sighed. "Tell your ma I will pray for her."

Meara nodded, then went off with her da.

Ma was speaking with Mrs. MacTavish, an elderly woman from our coven who'd been suffering from a hacking cough. As she spoke, I slipped away from Ma's side to find Kyra.

Gently I took my friend's arm and led her away from her ma and da. Feeling whimsical, I touched the stone in my pocket. "I have something for you," I said quietly. "Something to attract your certain someone."

She stared at me, uncomprehending.

I glanced around to make sure that none of the villagers were paying us any mind. Folks were engaged in the usual chatter, complaints of the long winter and worries over the spring planting. I turned back to Kyra. "Can you guess what's in my pocket?" When she shook her head, I whispered in her ear, "I've brought an amulet for you to attract Falkner."

Her cheeks grew pink at my words, and I wanted to laugh aloud. Kyra was so easy to embarrass. She took my hand and pulled me off the stone path, away from the churchgoers. "Would you have everyone in the Highlands hear of my secret love?"

"Harmless words," I said, adding in a whisper, "though I dare not show you the magickal gem before everyone in the village." The sun was still rising in the sky, promising a warm spring morning. Only days before, the last of the snow had melted from the ground. "Come with me to the woods," I said. "I need to collect herbs. We'll do the gathering ritual together, and afterward we'll charge the rose stone."

"Oh, I wish I could, but I promised Ma I would help with the baking." Kyra pressed a hand over her heart. "Are you sure the stone holds power?"

"Ma used to let me hold it whenever we quarreled. It's powerful enough."

Turning slightly, Kyra glanced toward the crowd still spilling out of the church. I knew she was looking for Falkner, a bean-pole of a boy who had yet to show any signs of intelligence in my presence. "Nothing seems to work on him," she said wistfully. "He can't even spare me a glance. It's as if I'm just a passing dragonfly, hardly worthy of notice."

I pressed my lips together, wishing that Kyra wouldn't go into it again. It was precisely the reason I had borrowed the rose stone from Ma's cupboard: to put an end to my friend's pining and suffering. "Come to the woods with me, then," I said.

"Kyra!" her mother called. Her parents were ready to leave.

She nodded at her ma respectfully, then tilted her head. "I cannot go," she told me regretfully. One chestnut braid slipped over her sapphire cloak. "But I do want the stone. Can you leave it on my doorstep? In a basket by the woodpile?"

"I dare not. It's too precious a thing to leave out."

"Rose . . ."

"Maybe tomorrow. Stop by our cottage on your way to market," I told her, wishing that Kyra could just once summon the courage to sneak away from her parents. She was my friend, but in every situation I was the bolder. While I dreamed of travel to distant places, of exploring and celebrating all corners of the Goddess's earth, Kyra was content to remain in her small world.

I went off to join my mother, who was getting an earful of unhappiness from Ian MacGreavy and his wife. Once we were out of earshot of the village, I told Ma of the failing health of Meara's mother.

"I fear she is not long with us." Ma shook her head. "'Tis a pity the Christians don't accept the Goddess's healing. I would like to help her."

A feeling of melancholy washed over me. "Poor Meara. She's already feeling the burden of so many chores to keep the children fed and clean."

"She shall forge ahead," Ma said stoutly.

I wondered if that had been Ma's attitude when my own father, Gowan MacEwan, had died. It made me sad that I barely remembered him, and whenever I asked about him, Ma went cold as the brook in winter. "Do you still miss Da?" I asked suddenly.

Ma sucked in a deep breath of crisp spring morning. "I will

always love him. But 'tis not a fit subject to discourse upon, especially when we have pressing matters at hand. The MacGreavys are in a tumult."

"Has the miller asked about dark magick again?" I asked, recalling how he had recently suggested calling on a taibhs, a dark spirit, to wreak vengeance against a Burnhyde man who had crossed him.

"As if we don't have enough trouble with the townspeople always on the lookout for witches," Ma said as we tramped down the rutted road to our cottage. "The tension among the Seven Clans is heating up again. Ian MacGreavy is outraged over a snub by a few men of the Burnhyde clan. Seems they won't use his mill, and they're telling all the others in their clan to avoid it, that it's cursed and the evil is spilling into the grain."

The unfairness of it irked me. "If the mill is cursed, it's because of a spell from one of them."

"Indeed. Mrs. MacGreavy found a sprinkling of soil and ashes on the threshold of the mill one morning, swirled in a circle."

"A spell wrought of minerals and soil . . ." Everyone knew that the Burnhyde witches were masters of spells involving crystals and minerals. "A sure sign that the Burnhydes are behind all their trouble."

"Aye, and trouble is rising for the MacGreavys. They fear the mill has been infested by rats." She pressed her lips together, and I could see from the bluish vein in her forehead that Ma was angry. "It's dark magick the Burnhydes are playing with."

"I can't believe it," I said, kicking at a dirt clod in the road. "This isn't about Ian MacGreavy's mill at all. It's about the other clans turning against the Wodebaynes again."

For as long as the Seven Great Clans had existed, there

had been strong rivalry among them. Everyone knew of the clans and their distinctions: the healing Braytindales, the master spellcrafters of the Wyndonkylles, the Burnhydes with their expertise in the use of crystals and metals. I had heard of the astute Ruanwandes, who were well schooled in all of the ways of the Goddess, though I had never met anyone from that clan. We knew of trickster Leapvaughns in neighboring villages, and everyone dreaded the war-loving Vykrothes, who were rumored to kick dirt in your face while passing you on the road. Aye, the clans had their reputations, the most slanderous being that of our own clan. For decades the other six clans had looked down upon our Wodebayne clan, their prejudice and hatred stinging like a wound that refused to heal.

Their hatred was prompted by a notion that Wodebaynes practiced dark magick. When a witch tried to harness the Goddess's power for evil purposes—to harm a living thing or to tamper with a person's free will—it was called dark magick. Other clans seemed to think that we Wodebaynes were expert at this black evil. They liked to blame their hardships on our "dark spells," and consequently they had grown to hate all Wodebaynes.

And now, as a result of that hatred, our own village mill was to be overrun by rats. "Can we help the MacGreavys to thwart the spell?"

Ma nodded. "The Burnhyde spell doesn't scare me, but their hatred of the Wodebaynes frightens me deep down in my bones."

Her worry spurred my anger. "Yet again we're back to the same hatred of the Wodebaynes. What did we do to bring on such animosity? Can you tell me that?"

"Easy, Rose."

"They act as if we were marauders and murderers! It's unfair!"

"Aye, it is," Ma said quietly. "But I have always said that the other clans will come to know us through our acts of goodness. The Goddess will reveal the true nature of the Wodebaynes in time."

"That doesn't help Ian MacGreavy, does it?" I asked.

"We will place a spell of protection around the mill," Ma said. "We'll do it tomorrow, on the full moon, the perfect time to cast a spell of protection. You'll need to collect sharp objects—old spearheads, broken darning needles—whatever you can find. They are to be stored in a jar, which we'll take to the mill."

As Ma went over the details of the spell of protection, I felt myself drifting off into an ocean of sorrow. My pitifully small world was growing smaller. With conflict among the clans heating up, we would be forced to become even more closed and guarded than we already were. Members of our coven would stick close to our hopelessly small country village, a tight knot of cottages that was already like a noose around my neck. Beyond my sweet but unadventurous friend Kyra, I was without a friend or possible mate within my own clan. No one outside the Wodebayne clan could be trusted, and any notions I'd ever had of exploration were squashed by the sure and steady evil lurking in new places.

Seventeen years of age, and already my life seemed to be over.

By now we had passed out of the village, which consisted mostly of the church, the mill, the inn, and a tangle of cottages that were built far too close to keep your business private. We came upon a flat, grassy field that was used by one of our own Wodebayne clansmen for herding his sheep, and indeed, two men were there at the edge of the field, talking to a sheep as if it had the sense in its head to understand and heed them.

The scene made me smile. The two men looked like bumblers, but Ma sucked in her breath, as if she'd just come upon a tragedy.

"What is it, Ma?" I asked.

She stopped walking, her hands crossed over her chest as she stared at the men, still not speaking.

"Aye, they could be punished," I observed. "Out on a Sunday, when work is to be set aside to praise the Christian Lord."

"If only they *would* meet with punishment," Ma said. "For thievery."

"What?" I ran ahead, then turned back to her to ask, "Who are they, Ma?"

"Vykrothe men," she said, reaching for my arm and holding it tightly.

Now that she said it, I could feel it. A blood witch can always sense other blood witches, and their presence was now palpable as a bracing cold wind. "Wait . . ." I said. "And now the Vykrothe men are stealing our Wodebayne sheep?" A sheep that would provide wool for spinning blankets and cloaks. A sheep whose slaughter would provide mutton to an entire family through many seasons. I tried to pull away from her. "We must stop them!"

She pulled me off the side of the road, behind the cover of a haystack. "Hush, child. Speak not your mind on this—the danger is too grave. We know not how strong their magick is, and they look much stronger than us physically."

"But—"

"I'll try to stop them." She lifted one hand, drawing a long circle around her body and then around mine. I couldn't hear the words she murmured, but I realized she was putting a cloaking spell upon us so that the Vykrothe men would not know we were blood witches.

Then Ma clasped her fingers through mine, locking me into place by her side as we stepped out of the shadow of the haystack and pressed ahead. I felt her fear, though I wasn't sure if she was frightened of the men or of my own desire to blast them. I pressed my lips together, determined to defer to my strong, noble mother on this.

"Good day to you, sirs," my mother called out to them.

They lifted their heads, mired in suspicion. "Good day," the taller man answered. His hooded eyes seemed sleepy, and he wore his flaxen hair pressed to his skull like a helmet.

"Did the sheep break loose?" Ma asked lightly. "They so often do, and I recognize that one as belonging to Thomas Draloose, who lives in the cottage just beyond the spring. I'll tell him of your act of kindness, returning his lost sheep to its pasture on this fine Sunday."

Act of kindness? I pressed Ma's arm, irked by the way she was coddling these tubs of lard.

But Ma went on. "It's noble of you, gentle sirs, taking the time, and—"

"This sheep is not returning to pasture, but departing," the tall Vykrothe said. "'Tis an evil beast, a harbinger of dark spirits. I know for true that this sheepherder you speak of is not a Christian man but a practitioner of witchcraft."

"You must be mistaken, sir!" Ma cried out.

"'Tis not a mistake at all," the shorter man insisted. He was a bull of a man, with so much flesh on his large bones, he could easily ram through a castle door. "This man is evil, a ghastly witch." He fixed his eyes on us menacingly. "Do you know him well?"

"Aye, I do," Ma answered boldly, "and I must proclaim his innocence of such ungodly pursuits."

The taller Vykrothe yanked on the rope. "Proclaim what you will. We must remove this sheep before it turns into a demon."

Ma shook her head and gave a fake laugh. "A mere sheep, sir? It is but an animal. One of the Lord's creatures, is it not?"

I gave Ma's hand a squeeze. The man could hardly argue with Christian philosophy.

The tall Vykrothe leaned closer, and his unpleasant smell of sweat, dung, and sour cheese rankled the air. "This sheep is possessed. I have seen it bleat at the moon, its eyes red with Satan's fires."

"Aye," Ma countered, "and what reason have you to be lurking in a stranger's fields at night?"

The tall man leaned back, but the bull answered, "And I've heard rumor that the herder is planning to spill its blood in a dreadful spell of harm and destruction." He turned to his friend, dropped his voice to a whisper, and added, "Just like those Wodebaynes."

I felt my fists clenching at the muttered slander. He had thought we would not hear or understand his strike against our clan and likely didn't care that we did since he thought us to be Christian women. But I had heard, and my blood boiled at the insult. These men weren't even common sheep thieves—they were bigots, striking out against one of our own.

"This, sir, I must dispute," my mother said. She sounded so sincere, so earnest. How could these men refuse to believe her? "Do you imply that all Wodebaynes are evil?"

When Ma spoke the word, the bullish man took two steps back. "What Christian woman knows so much of evil?" the man accused.

"How dare you speak to her that way!" I shouted. My fingers twitched with the urge to shoot dealan-dé at him and burn him with its flinty blue sparks. But Ma was already pulling me down the road, her other arm having slid protectively around my waist.

"Make haste," she whispered in my ear, "lest they raise their ire toward us. The Vykrothes are known to love war, and raise arms they will."

"But the sheep . . ." I gasped. "They're stealing it . . . and even talking of witchcraft could get Thomas Draloose and his family hanged."

"Hush, child." Ma hurried me along, pressing her head down against mine. "We must choose our battles. I did my best to defend Thomas and save the sheep, but we cannot always win against such cruelty."

"It's unfair," I said, feeling tears sting my eyes. "Why do they hate the Wodebaynes so?"

"I cannot say, child," Ma whispered. "I cannot say."

2.

Gathering and Sanctifying Spring Herbs

That afternoon I collected my gathering basket, retrieved my bolline from its hiding place in the seat of one of our wooden chairs, and set off to collect the newest herbs of spring. I knew many small trails through the woods; tiny lanes and hidden paths that led to my favorite gathering places.

A few years ago, when I was around the age of ten, Ma had agreed to let me gather the first herbs on my own. Since then it had been a ritual I performed gladly, grateful for the peace of mind it offered and for the thread of power that laced itself up from the plants through my fingertips. Aye, the feeling of power was sweet when it came my way, though it didn't happen to me often enough in the coven circle.

Sometimes I worried that I had fallen in the shadow of my mother, that somehow Ma was interceding and collecting my blessings until she thought I was ready to deal directly with the Goddess. An odd belief, I know, but I had my reasons. For one, Ma had never given me a significant role at Sabbats. And she constantly questioned me when I returned from the woods, having performed a spell or consecration in a solitary circle. She said it was her duty to educate me in the ways of the Goddess, but I sensed that she didn't trust me. And why was that? When I was on my own, I felt a strong connection to the Goddess, and I had always quested to grow in my craft. Why, then, did my own mother question my devotion?

"She's just your ma, doing what mothers do," Kyra always told me. Perhaps she was right. Perhaps Ma didn't realize how difficult it was to be the daughter of a high priestess.

Birds chirped in the woods as I swung my basket gently. I'd spent many a winter's eve sewing pouches of sapphire blue, ruby red, and saffron cloth in preparation for this day. A different pouch for each herb, enough to replenish our supplies. Of course, back at the cottage the herbs would need to be dried in the rafters and eventually ground, but this was my favorite part of the ritual— gathering under the crown of trees and the canopy of blue sky.

I followed the path until I came to my solitary circle, a small natural clearing with a large, gray stone that I'd cleansed for use as an altar. Beside a tall oak was my broom, modestly constructed of twigs and a long stick I'd rubbed smooth with the help of a rough stone. I placed my gathering basket on the altar, then began to sweep the circle, swinging my broom as I walked slowly. The spell I chanted was my own, one that I'd created years ago. Ma had once called it primitive and childish, which wounded me deeply, yet I clung to the spell. It had come from my heart, and I always felt that the Goddess heard it and answered favorably.

> "Sweep, sweep this circle for me,
> By powers of wind, so mote it be."

My circle complete, I placed the broom at the gateway and closed my eyes. A gentle current of air stirred around me—the breath of the Goddess. I lingered long enough to breathe it in, my breast swelling with the wind. Then I lifted my hands and face to the sun.

> *"Light, light this circle for me,*
> *By powers of fire, so mote it be."*

Warmth shot through my body, from the crown of my head down through my heart. The Goddess was with me today, her power so strong. Reeling with a vivid feeling of life, I lifted the tiny flask of consecrated water from my basket and sprinkled it around my circle.

> *"Water, cleanse this circle for me,*
> *By the powers of water, so mote it be."*

As I stood in the center of the circle, I imagined water flowing around me. My skirts swirled at the center of the tidepool, and the tang of fresh spring water cleansed my throat.

Oh, Goddess, you are with me today. I feel your presence. I treasure it.

I sank to my knees, scraping both hands at the ground beside me. Lifting my hands, I let the soil whisper to the ground as I chanted:

> *"Dirt, bless this circle for me,*
> *By the powers of earth, so mote it be."*

The sun seemed to shine brighter, a lemony halo of light favoring my circle. I thanked the Goddess for lending me Her power, then went to the altar to cleanse and consecrate my basket, my pouches, my knife. I realized I felt lighter, buoyed by Her power. Whatever had been bogging me down earlier had dissipated, turned to dust and carried off in the wind at the Goddess's touch.

Now to set about collecting herbs.

I left the circle and ventured off to a thicket I'd known to produce a variety of plants. My first harvest was a bay plant, a hearty green stem with fat, dark leaves. Gathering my skirts and tucking them between my legs, I crouched beside the plant and pressed the blade of my bolline into the soil.

"Thank you, Goddess, for this beautiful herb," I said, drawing a circle around the plant to protect its energy. Then, cutting off the heartiest sprigs, I thanked the plant for its usefulness as a poultice for ailments of the chest. Ma also used bay leaves in spells of protection, though I'd yet to try this. When I was finished, the plant bounced back jovially, and I felt confident it would thrive and go on to produce many more harvests.

I moved on to other plants—anise for treatment of colic, thyme to rid internal disorders, clover to conjure money, love, and luck. Each time I did a cutting, I repeated the ritual, drawing a circle with my bolline, thanking the Goddess, soothing the plant. My basket was filling. I leaned close to a fennel plant, my bolline held in midair as I wondered whether the plant would be best harvested later.

The forest was silent.

The birds had stopped chirping.

And I sensed that I was not alone.

I froze in place. My heartbeat thundered in my ears as I realized I was holding the bolline—the very same object that had incriminated poor Fionnula. I could be tried as a witch for this gathering ritual, tried and jailed and sentenced to death. Quickly I shoved the bolline into the basket, burying it under the fresh-cut herbs.

Fear-stricken, I clenched the basket and tried to calm myself. Perhaps the intruder had not noticed me yet. With luck, he or she was too far away to spy the runes carved into the handle of my bolline. I wondered if I should cast a blocking spell over myself . . . or a spell of protection. But there was no time.

Say that you're gathering herbs, I thought. The task of gathering herbs is totally innocent.

Unless the intruder finds your tool of witchcraft.

I turned to confront the enemy.

And the enemy smiled at me. 'Twas a tall, solid boy, not much older than myself, and for a moment I wondered if the Goddess had sent him on a jagged bolt of lightning. Even from across the clearing his blue eyes flashed with that intensity, like the night sky lit during a storm.

Clasping the basket to my breast, I closed my eyes, then opened them, sure he would vanish just as readily as he had appeared. He did not. Instead he came toward me, reaching up to grab an overhanging branch, then swinging closer. He landed a short space away from me, his ginger brown hair falling over one eye.

"Did I startle you?" he asked.

"No . . . aye, that is . . ." I fumbled for words, sensing that he was not a threat, at least not in the way I had feared. For my immediate sense was that he held power . . . not the power to persecute, but the grand, sweeping power possessed only by a blood witch. A blood witch, but from what clan? Certainly not a Wodebayne, as Síle's coven included every living Wodebayne within miles.

"What's that, then?" he teased. "Do you think it wise for a lass like yourself to wander these woods alone?"

"I wander these woods often, gathering herbs," I said, trying to draw out our encounter with conversation. "Though I've not seen you leaping from trees."

"I trust you've not seen many lads leaping from trees," he said, hooking a thumb over his leather belt.

"You're my first, I must admit."

"Well, that's certainly an honor. I'd imagine men would go to battle to be your first." That he would imply something so intimate nearly stole my breath away. He spoke the words of a man, but the humor in his eyes was boyish and full of youth. The drawstrings of his white shirt were open at the throat, revealing a fair amount of skin turned tawny from the sun. More skin than most men laid bare, except in circles. I wondered what he would look like in a circle, his robe slipping away from those broad, tanned shoulders.

I have met my match, I thought, letting the basket drop to one arm.

Aye, he was handsome from head to toe, and his conversation had a certain cleverness that amused. But those qualities merely added to my enchantment. I was drawn to him—inexorably, irrevocably drawn to the power that swirled around him like a visiting wind.

At that moment, I didn't know where he had come from or

where he was headed, but with grave certainty I knew that I wanted to be the one to accompany him in his travels. I longed to move close to him and slide the tunic off his shoulders, touch the wall of his chest. And how would it feel to be touched by such a god . . . the sweet press of his lips upon mine, the shimmer of his hands over my body? I slid one hand into the pocket of my skirt and clenched the rose stone. If ever a spell were necessary, this was the time. But what were the words?

He turned and reached up to swing from the tree limb again, giving me a chance to conjure a quick spell.

I set my mind on the power I had felt swirling in my circle. *Oh, Goddess.* I felt the stone's power swelling in my palm, like a quickly blossoming flower. *Thank You for bringing him to me. Let him ever be drawn to me, as a man to a woman, ever in love. Ever after.*

The warmth of the stone rippled up my arm and passed on through my body. I let out a gasp of shock and joy, though I think he was too caught up in showing off his climbing skills to notice. Then he turned toward me and stared.

He stared at me as if he'd only just discovered the answer to his lifelong quest.

My heart clamored with joy that the Goddess had heard me. The magickal stone was now charmed, and we were under its spell.

He slid down from the tree and rubbed his hands on his breeches. "I fear I am more lost than I realized. I thought I had strayed from the path and discovered a maiden, but I was mistaken. I seem to have wandered into an enchanted faerie world, into the realm of a dark, tiny wood nymph. A beauty with glistening black hair and eyes that hold the secrets of the night."

I smiled, feeling myself blossom at his words. I had always

viewed myself as small and plain, unworthy of much notice for my appearance. It delighted me to hear myself described so. "You are too kind. I am but a village girl, gathering herbs to make a pottage."

He lifted the basket from my hand. "Bay leaves . . . anise for colic. Thyme to aid in digestion. And clover . . ." He pulled the basket away, teasing me. "These are enchanted herbs, my lady. Tell me, where does your circle gather?"

"I know not of a circle, but for the shape of the full moon," I lied, reaching for my basket. But he stopped my hand with his own, and suddenly we were touching, the sensitive palms of our hands aligned like the stars of a splendid constellation.

His lips moved, forming no words, but his glittering blue eyes told a tale of surprise and desire.

And love? Had my spell worked? I looked into his eyes, begging the question.

His answer was the brush of his lips against mine, a gentle surprise followed by a rich, ripe kiss. I kissed him back, reveling in the feel of his lips on mine, rejoicing in the power that hummed when we touched. This was a passion matched only by the incredible spark I had felt in my solitary circle, and I knew at once that the Goddess was here with us. The Goddess had brought us together. It was meant to be.

And from the way his fingers gently cupped my cheek and followed the line of my jaw to my hair, from the way he held my arm securely as if he would never let go, it was clear that he knew it, too.

He squeezed my arm, letting out a small laugh. "The sun is falling. I'll be on the road after nightfall, but I can't bring myself to care . . . or to leave."

Nightfall. Danger. Looking to the west, I saw only the orange-and-purple glow above the tree line. "I must go, too. But I cannot say good-bye. I can't bear it." My eyes were level with the open ties of his shirt, where a gold pentagram dangled on a leather cord. I reached out and touched it brazenly. In turn, he pressed a finger below the crook of my neck, just above my breasts.

"It will be yours," he whispered. "For I am yours already."

It was a startling admission, coming from a boy I'd only just met. I thought of the boys I had known in my life. None had ever sparked a flame of interest within me, despite a few awkward kisses and groping hands. More than once Meara and I had encountered village boys down by the brook. They were gawky, rough-hewn creatures who teased and chased us, always wanting to steal off into the woods with one of us. More than once I'd had to kick one of them away. Neither boy nor man had held any appeal for me.

Until now.

"Come to me tomorrow," he said, holding my hands to his chest. "Meet me here, at the same time. Please say you will."

"I will," I promised, loving the way my slender fingers disappeared in his large, warm hands. He kissed my fingertips, then backed away, walking awkwardly into the woods.

"You're going to hit your head," I called, gesturing for him to turn around.

"But I can't take my eyes from you," he said.

"Then I must vanish." I hitched up my skirts and raced out of the clearing, resolved not to turn back lest I linger in his arms forevermore. I was breathless from running and from his kisses, but I kept it up, slipping over a patch of dried mud and ignoring the brambles that caught at my stockings. I would run through the heather without shoes, roll down the rocky hills headfirst if it would get me closer to him.

In my deepest heart, I knew that I had met my mùirn beatha dàn—my only soul mate. I did not yet know his name. I knew only that he was mine.

I pressed my hand to the side of my skirt, feeling the weight and warmth of the rose stone through my pocket.

Astounding, I realized, the power of a charmed gem.

Even more surprising was the power of my own spell. I hadn't been quite sure of the magnitude of the power—of my power—when I had planned to spell the stone for Kyra. But by the grace of the Goddess, the amulet had brought me love.

3.
Charging an Amulet, Esbat, Seed Moon

The next morning I went about the cottage, performing my usual chores with a lightness in my heart, as if a heavy burden had been lifted. Suddenly it did not seem at all tedious to clean the cabin and air the linens and stoke the fire in preparation for breaking fast.

And the last eve I hadn't minded when Ma had questioned me about the herbs I had gathered, nor when I was chastised about the dangers of returning home after sunset. I did not think she had believed my story about the herbs being sparse and difficult to find, and I could feel her eyes upon me, watching curiously. No doubt she was surprised by my suddenly blithe spirit.

As was I. The meeting in the woods had changed everything about my dull, suffocating life. Suddenly the Goddess had filled the very air around me with beauty, and the sure knowledge that I would see him again doubled the pleasure in each moment till then.

When Kyra arrived, I was eager to go off with her and tell

her everything. And from the way she switched from one foot to the other, I could see she was equally anxious. Likely eager for her love amulet, which she didn't know the half about.

"I must take some biscuits over to the market at Kirkloch," Kyra said, resting a heavy basket on the table inside the cottage. Kirkloch was a nearby Christian village with a small marketplace and a blacksmith. "Ma and Da were hoping you would go along. Otherwise Ma will put off her spinning and go with me."

"May I go?" I asked my mother. I was already untying my apron and brushing soot from my skirt. "I've finished my chores."

But Ma was not so agreeable. "After our encounter with those thieves yesterday, I am not sure it's safe. And what of the preparations for tonight's Esbat?" Her arms crossed, Ma watched me with suspicion. Since tonight was the full moon, our coven would gather in the woods for an Esbat—a meeting of witches. We would worship the Goddess and take care of coven matters such as spells and charms. "Have you gathered what we need for the spell over the mill?"

"No, not yet." I wiped my moist palms on my skirt.

"Then you cannot go. Not when you can't be trusted to complete your chores and be home before sunset." I couldn't believe she was issuing such an edict, but she simply turned back to her spinning, as if I were being punished. Aye, perhaps she was punishing me for glowing with the Goddess's joy. Sometimes it was impossible to understand my mother.

"But Ma . . ."

"Please, ma'am," Kyra beseeched her.

"I've made my decision, and that is that!" Ma snapped. Although she didn't bother to look at me, her anger was palpable.

The breath rushed out of Kyra as she gave me a desperate look.

I knew I had to get out of the cottage before my news burst forth like a cinder popping out of the fire. "The sharp objects I need for the spell," I said, thinking aloud. "I've a good chance of finding things like that along the roadside. Broken spearheads and pointed stones and such."

My mother stopped spinning, considering.

"And there's the blacksmith's shop," I said. "He is sure to have some discarded metals and arrowheads."

"Please?" Kyra added.

Ma touched her forehead. "At least you're thinking like a witch now."

"And we'll be back in plenty of time for Esbat," I said. After dark our coven would gather to celebrate April's seed moon. It was a time to banish unwanted influences and cast spells of protection—a perfect time to help the MacGreavys out of their dilemma.

"All right, then, you may go," my mother relented. "But do not forget your chores. I'll not have the MacGreavys without a spell of protection because a daughter of mine neglected her duties."

"Aye, Ma," I said, feeling once again like the put-upon daughter of the high priestess. I hated it, but often I felt as if I did the work while she got the glory.

I grabbed my veil and cloak, not daring to stay to question my mother's change of heart. The rose stone was in my pocket, a glimmering reminder of the fantastical spell I had conjured, and though I had promised it to Kyra, I was now afraid to part with it. Hence I had sneaked into Ma's cabinet that morning and found a stone that might do just as well for Kyra—a pale green moonstone, which was known to promote love and compassion.

Before we reached the end of the path, I told Kyra of my meeting in the woods and of the splendid spell the Goddess had given me. As I spoke, her mouth opened, her jaw dropping in amazement.

"A kiss!" Her hand flew to her face. "You let a stranger kiss you?"

"Not a stranger," I said confidently. "He's a blood witch. My mùirn beatha dàn—I'm sure of it."

"Who could he be?" Kyra wondered. "And from what clan?"

"I'll learn his name and clan today. We're meeting this afternoon," I said, smiling at the promise of seeing the sparkle of his eyes again. Reaching into my pocket, I took out the rose stone and held it up to the sky. It glimmered and winked in the sunlight.

"That's the rose stone?" Kyra asked, staring at it. "Oh, by the Goddess, it does exude power."

While I dreamed of meeting him again, Kyra went on and on with dire warnings. How I should not trust a stranger. How I must beware anyone from another coven. How it was wrong to lie to my ma. How I shouldn't have charmed the stone in the first place.

"Aye, but you had no objection when it was to be spelled for you," I pointed out.

"You're right." She flipped a braid over her shoulder and sighed. "I'm a fool in love, and now I've even lost my chance at having an amulet."

"Don't despair." I took the moonstone from my pocket

and presented it to her with a flourish. "This stone promotes love and sympathy. And I heard one of the coven witches go on about its magickal ability to melt a lovers' quarrel. It helps to open up emotions between two lovers."

Kyra's face turned pink. "But Falkner and I are not lovers!"

"Ah, but you shall be," I teased in a singsongy voice. "Come, we'll stop at my circle and charge the moonstone for you."

My circle in the woods was on the way to Kirkloch, and Kyra had been there before for gathering and practicing spells of our own. Kyra always deferred to me, as we both knew my powers with the Goddess were strong. Of late, some of Síle's coveners had seemed to notice my powers. Once while Síle was drawing down the moon, coveners saw a halo of light surround me. Me—not the high priestess. My body had trembled with life force that night, but Ma had barely said a word beyond reminding me to ground myself when the rites ended. Sometimes I truly believed she was envious of my powers.

I swept the circle with my broom, cleansing it for the spell. Then I placed the moonstone upon the altar and joined hands with Kyra.

"Do you want to put the spell on your charm?" I asked her.

"Would you do it for me?" She turned to me, her dark eyes beseeching. "You have so strong a bond with the Goddess, I think it's best coming from you. Everyone knows you're to be the next high priestess when Síle steps down."

I squeezed her hand, feeling flattered. "I don't know that everyone has accepted that just yet. My own ma questions my spells and whereabouts every minute of every day."

"She's trying to teach you."

"Well, if chastisement and disapproval are teaching, I'll not be her student." I went to the altar, where the moonstone sat in the dappled sunlight. Ma always said spells were best cast at night, and it was certainly safer, but it was nearly impossible to steal off and make magick under the moonlight with her watching me as she did. After making certain we were alone, I bowed to the Goddess, asking for Her blessing over this stone. As always, I summoned the power of earth, wind, water, and fire. Then I turned and handed the moonstone to Kyra.

"Hold it next to the pounding in your breast," I told her.

She pressed the stone to the bodice of her gown.

I felt the power above me. Lifting my chin, I saw the moon in the sky through a clearing in the circle. It was full and visible today, thrumming with life force and power. So much power for tonight's Esbat. I went to my stash of tools and took out my athame, a long wand I'd made from a tree branch and a lovely pointed stone I'd spied in the river. Standing in the center of the circle, the athame in my right hand, I felt the moon trembling in the crown over the trees. I raised my arms directly above me and clasped them both at the base of the athame.

"I now draw the power of the moon into myself," I said, "merging with her power, the pure essence of the Goddess." My breath came sharp and fast as the moon flashed onto the tip of my athame. I could feel it there, coursing down onto the sharp stone. I let the moon fill the athame, then brought the tool down and pressed its sharp tip to my chest.

At once the power danced through me. Molten silver filled my breast, my body, my whole being. Beside me I heard Kyra gasp, but I could not turn my head to look over, so engrossed was I in drawing down the moon.

When I was fully saturated, I swung around and pointed my athame at Kyra, touching her chest to let the power soar into her. Her dark eyes reflected the silver light as she watched it stream through my athame.

"In this day and in the hour I call upon thee, ancient power." I spoke slowly, steadily. "Kyra has a need that must be met, a true love to draw to her, Falkner to call for her. Charm this stone, O Goddess of Light. Bring her love to cherish and delight."

The spell complete, I pulled the athame away and dropped to the ground, pulling Kyra along beside me. I had learned from coven circles that so much power could sap a witch, making the head light and the body weak. Grounding was essential.

After a few moments Kyra sat up, blowing dirt from her hands. "The Goddess has truly blessed you, Rose," she said. "The way you summon Her power, 'tis like a circle with the elders, who have so much more experience."

"The power runs in my blood," I said, neither bragging nor awed by it. I had come to accept that my destiny was intertwined with the Goddess, even if my own ma wasn't nearly so sure.

It seemed like hours had passed drawing down the moon, but the sun was still high in the clear sky. Carefully I hid away my tools, and we returned to the road to Kirkloch.

When we reached the gathering of cottages at the edge of Kirkloch, Kyra resolved to go directly to the market, but I would not have it.

"We must stop at the blacksmith first," I insisted. "I have grave need of sharp objects for tonight's spell of protection."

Her cheeks turned pink. "Aye, and whose father happens to be the blacksmith of Kirkloch?"

It was none other than Falkner, I knew. "I'm here to help you get beyond your fears," I teased her. "Where would you be without me, Kyra? Hiding in your cottage, under your ma's skirts?"

"I would not," she insisted, but she came close and kissed my cheek lightly. "But you're a good friend, Rose MacEwan. A good friend indeed."

I smiled, sure that our destinies were to be filled with love and happiness. It was such a good feeling after the heaviness that had fallen upon me of late, the pressing danger of persecution from the Christians, the unfair hatred from every rival clan. I took Kyra's hand and skipped ahead merrily.

"I'll drop my basket!" she protested, laughing.

"Well, then, hold on tight," I said as I pulled her along. Outside the blacksmith's shop, I let her compose herself before we ducked around the post and faced the blaring heat of the fires under the overhang. There was the usual wild flurry of activity as the blacksmiths clanged and banged horseshoes and the like, sparks flying and fires hissing. It brought to mind the many times I had accompanied Kyra here and, indeed, to other places in pursuit of her beloved Falkner, who now stood off to the side, prodding the fire with a long poker. How many times had I encouraged her to speak to him, to smile at him, to call his name? All to no avail. He usually gave her a frightened look, then skulked away.

But today would be different.

By the power of the Goddess, my Kyra would have her boy's love.

"Touch the moonstone," I whispered to Kyra.

Reflexively she pressed a finger to her neck, where she'd strung the stone onto a piece of twine. Her eyes flashed to Falkner, who looked up from the fire . . .

And dropped his poker.

It was as if he'd never seen Kyra before. His heat-ruddy face went pale as he ignored the poker and crossed over to the railing where we stood. Kyra lowered her eyes, but her huge smile revealed her interest as she greeted him and offered a biscuit. Falkner accepted gratefully but didn't take his eyes off her as he lifted the morsel to his mouth and took a bite.

I clapped a hand to my cheek, thrilled that the charm was working.

Blessed be. All thanks to your power, sweet Goddess.

Falkner and Kyra were still gazing at each other when Falkner's father, a witch in our coven, finished with a customer and bade us good day. "And who's been baking here?" he asked. I knew John Radburn from many a circle. He was a jovial man, far more spirited than his son.

"I baked with my ma," Kyra said, lifting the cloth to offer him a biscuit.

He took one and set it aside on a tin plate. "That'll go nicely with my beer at midday, thank you. And what can I help you with, lassies?"

"We came to trade the biscuits at the market," I said. "But while I'm here, do you mind me poking about to find leftover sharp objects? Ma needs them to . . . to scare off the crows from her garden," I lied. Blacksmith Radburn probably knew of the spell of protection to be cast at the mill, but it wouldn't do to have strangers overhear talk of our magick.

"Help yourself." The blacksmith moved the toe of his boot through the dirt to reveal a few jagged pieces of metal. He picked them up and set them on the rail before me. "But mind you don't touch anything that's still heated."

"I'll take care, sir," I said, slipping the sharp items into a thick pouch.

The blacksmith turned back to his work, and I set to searching the ground for sharps. Falkner helped me a bit as he chatted with Kyra; then he, too, returned to tend the fires. When I had a pouch full of splintered nails and shards and arrowheads, Kyra and I thanked the blacksmith and headed away.

Falkner gave an excited nod of farewell, as if Kyra had just brought him a priceless gift.

She squeezed my arm as we made our way toward the market. "Did you see? Your spell worked. The charm is drawing his love!"

"Of course it worked," I said. "You cannot doubt the Goddess."

"No, but I have doubted how strongly one could be connected to Her. Until now. You have summoned Her power to bring me love! Oh, Rose, 'tis the most wondrous thing!"

"Aye." I thought of my mystery boy. I still didn't even know his name.

"And I'll see Falkner tonight at Esbat circle. And at every circle. And from now on, when he looks at me, he'll truly see me instead of staring right through me. What could be better?"

"Which reminds me of my appointed meeting this afternoon. Let's make haste at the market so we can return quickly."

Kyra nodded. "I'll sell the biscuits to a vendor, and we'll head home." As she negotiated with merchants at the market, I wandered past carts of brightly colored ribbons, mutton pies, fresh fruits and vegetables. A small black pig squealed as children chased it through the maze of carts. It squeezed past a stout woman's skirts and darted toward the churchyard.

I turned back to the vegetable cart, my fingers pinching a potato. Was it worth the price to thicken our Esbat stew? I could sense that the vendor was a blood witch. Glancing up, I saw that he was eyeing me suspiciously.

"An odd thing, the potato," came a familiar voice. "When digging in the dirt, one has to wonder, is it something to eat or a stone to be cast away?"

My heart sang as I swung around to sparkling blue eyes. It was my boy!

"Aye, sir, I would not eat a stone, but these would do well in a stew," I said, holding two potatoes out to him.

"Hmmm. Or for a jester's tricks." He took the two potatoes and began to toss them, juggling them aptly.

"What's that, now!" the vendor growled. "I'll not have you ruining my wares, boy!" The man, sporting a dense brown beard and red nose, came around his cart, stamping a foot at my love.

"Easy, kind sir." My boy stopped his juggling and held out the potatoes. "I've not damaged them in the least."

The vendor looked angrily from him to me, his eyes narrowing as he took in my petite stature and dark coloring. "And you were touching them." He leaned close to growl softly at me, "You're a Wodebayne, are you not?"

"I am," I answered truthfully, astonished as I was that he would dare speak openly of clans and covens in public. I turned to my boy, wondering if he had heard. Did he know that I was a Wodebayne, one of the so-called evil ones? If he had heard, he did not seem daunted by the fact. He studied the vendor with a mixture of distaste and curiosity.

"Then *you*," groused the vendor, nearly breathing down my neck, "are not permitted to touch my merchandise. How do I know you haven't cast a dark spell upon my wares so that the person who eats them will come down with a racking cough? Or a hideous boil. Or mayhap a burning fever!"

My senses stirred with alarm at his attack. The only consolation was that this man, whatever his clan, would not want to raise the hackles of the people in this Christian village. "Sir, I do not cast harmful spells," I said softly.

"That's what all your kind say," the vendor growled again, suddenly aware that the villagers were taking notice.

All around us it seemed as though people had stopped their business and conversation to watch. I could feel the crowd closing in, watching, waiting. The witches among them were probably hoping the Wodebayne girl would get her comeuppance, as usual. I felt a tightness in my throat, not so much at the disapproval of the crowd as that my boy should be dragged through such turmoil. And surely the hatred of Wodebaynes would frighten him away.

"Just a moment!" the boy interrupted, holding the potatoes high in his hands. He lifted them, weighing and measuring with some degree of drama. "They do not speak, and I see no cryptic message carved among their bruises. There is truly no charm here," he told the vendor. "But the potatoes must certainly be far more delicious for having been touched by a lovely maiden's hands."

A few people laughed, and he nodded at them, his cheekbones high and taut above his broad grin. The crowd began to turn away. Somehow my boy had diffused the swell of hatred against me.

The vendor folded his arms across his chest, still not satisfied.

"I must insist, sir, that you let me purchase these potatoes—these two, no others shall do—for I find that I cannot leave this market without them."

The vendor took a coin from the boy and crept back behind his cart.

"Thank you, sir. A pleasure doing business with you," the boy called. He turned away and handed me the potatoes. "My gift to you. Though it can hardly make up for the way that ogre tried to defame you."

"His hatred does not surprise me," I said. "I've come to expect it, though I don't know that I'll ever become accustomed to it." I dropped the two potatoes into my skirt pockets, where they bounced against my hips.

He watched with awe and reverence. "Would that I could venture where they go," he said huskily.

I laughed at the temerity of his words, here in the wide-open marketplace. "Aren't you the daring one?" I said. "When you're not swinging from trees in the forest, you rescue Wodebayne maidens from mad crowds, then dream of their skirts."

He shrugged and eyed me merrily. "And you despise me for that?"

I looked up at his handsome face and felt the rhythm of my life force increasing. "No, no, on the contrary."

"Rose!" Kyra called, summoning me. "We must go!"

"Rose?" he repeated. "Like the rose on the bush, gentle and sweet, yet ready to prick a finger when approached the wrong way?"

" 'Tis I."

He lowered his head, his hair falling over his eyes in a shroud of secrecy. "We will talk later, Rose."

I nodded, trying to remember every detail of his sultry looks, his feathery light brown hair, his sky blue eyes, his broad shoulders and long legs, coltish yet strong.

With a deep breath I turned away and joined Kyra, who had apparently witnessed the scene with the irate vendor.

"I was so frightened for you!" she said. "What do you think the man wanted? Would he have you locked in jail because you touched his wares? Everyone examines merchandise before trading."

I shook my head, feeling a sense of warm, tender love. It wrapped around me like a cloak of security, just knowing that my boy cared for me, was willing to fight for me. "The man was full of Wodebayne hatred. I don't know what clan he was from, but did you see what happened? The way my boy rescued me? He is the boy I've spoken of. He is a hero. My hero."

"I'm not sure of that," Kyra said regretfully. "Falkner knows him, Rose. His name is Diarmuid, and he's a Leapvaughn. Not one of us."

"Diarmuid," I said, treasuring the sound of his name. I repeated it over and over in my mind.

"He cannot be your true love, Rose. Falkner and I both fear for your heart. He'll hate you as much as his clan hates Wodebaynes."

"Aye, but he doesn't. That's the blessing of the Goddess. It doesn't matter if he's Leapvaughn or Braytindale or Wyndonkylle. He has a good heart. Diarmuid doesn't hate without reason. Didn't you see? He defended me from that peddler. I ought to toss that old ogre's potatoes into the brook!"

"He was a terrible man!" Kyra pressed her hand to her throat, touching her charmed moonstone. "I'll agree Diarmuid did save you. I'll grant you that, and he is a handsome lad. Falkner says he's not of Kirkloch. Where does he live, Rose?"

"That I don't know, but I shall find out. I must cherish this gift from the Goddess."

Kyra shook her head. "But he cannot be a gift from the Goddess, Rose. Not a Leapvaughn boy."

"Would you stop saying that? I'll not allow you to be so small-minded!"

"But to get involved with someone from another clan . . ."

"I know." The reality of it stabbed at me. Diarmuid and I would have to face more than our share of foes. But as I walked along, my mother's words came back to me. She always said that the other clans would one day see the good in the Wodebaynes.

Perhaps I had been chosen to help the world see our goodness.

It lifted my spirits to know that Diarmuid already saw the goodness within me. I couldn't wait to see him again.

Kyra walked alongside me, observing. "You look more in love now than before you knew he was not one of us. But then, you've always been stubborn, Rose MacEwan."

"Aye," I said, thinking of Diarmuid's eyes, his suggestive words, his strong jaw. "I think the Goddess has a plan," I told Kyra. "And I won't let anyone meddle with Her gift to me. I will not be daunted."

4.

Drawing Down the Moon

"It worries me, Rose. I know you think you can fight your own battles, but sometimes I fear for you, my child." My mother scrubbed the potatoes furiously, upset by what had happened in the market at Kirkloch.

Of course, I hadn't given her all the details of the story. I'd said that Diarmuid was a traveling peddler, probably a Wodebayne from the north. And although I hadn't mentioned that some in the crowd seemed eager to join in on the Wodebayne bashing, I think she got the complete picture. Whether through her inner sight or simply her experience, Ma had spent her lifetime enduring prejudice from others.

"But it's over, Ma," I reassured her. "'Twas over soon after it began, and we got two fine potatoes out of it."

She turned away, her face in shadow so that I could not see more than the hollows of her eyes. "I'll thank the Goddess for my supper, not some brash vendor with hatred in his heart." Her voice was strained, and I thought I saw a spot on her cheek—a dark tear. Was she crying?

"What is it, Ma?"

She shook her head. Her chopping was done. "This hatred of the Wodebaynes has to end, Rose. I had hoped it would subside during your youth, but instead it seems to be rising like a river during the spring rains."

I wanted to tell her that the prejudice against us didn't bear down on me so heavily now, not since I'd met Diarmuid. He was a window of light, my escape from the dark hatred that seemed to be closing in around the Wodebaynes. I wanted to go to her and touch her shoulder and ease her pain. . . .

But I couldn't. I knew that talk of a boy, especially a boy from another clan, would rattle Ma all the more. And I feared that if I touched her, if I rested my head on her shoulder or squeezed her arm, she would know the truth.

That the Goddess had interceded, bringing her daughter true love.

I went to her and scooped the potatoes onto my apron, then dropped them into the cauldron over the fire. Already the savory smells of tomato and herbs and beans rose from the kettle.

"The moon is full already," I said, eager to change the subject. "You can see it in the day sky, hanging large as you please." I stirred the stew, talking over my shoulder. "I'd like to go off and draw it down, Ma." Again, a lie, but what could I do?

" 'Tis the seed moon," she said. "We'll have a fine Esbat tonight."

I stepped away from the fire and took off my apron. "I've gathered what we need for tonight's spell. John Radburn was helpful."

She nodded. "You can go. But don't be long. We've a few chores to do before the circle."

I moved slowly, trying to ignore the coursing sound in my ears that urged me to make haste and run off to meet Diarmuid. I hung my apron on the rail outside, measuring my steps while I was in view of our cottage.

One, two, three . . . four steps closer to him.

The waiting was excruciating.

At last I reached the brush at the end of the path. Without looking back, I scooped up my skirts and leapt ahead, startling a small rabbit from the heather at the side of the trail. It darted off into the brush, and I laughed. "I'll not hurt you, little one," I called, racing ahead.

By the time I neared our meeting place, my neck and hands were damp with sweat. I slowed my pace to a brisk walk, mopping my neck with a rough cloth from my pocket. It reminded me that the rose stone was still there, and I paused to take it in my hand and hold it up to the glowing day moon.

"I thank thee, Goddess, for the use of thy power."

When I lowered my hands, the stone winked at me, ever cheerful and appealing. I lifted the top of my dress and dropped the stone down into the hollow between my breasts. Its warm glow worked its magick there, emanating from the middle of my body like a ray of sunshine breaking through clouds.

"Rose?"

It was him. He appeared directly before me, slipping from the trees as though he had materialized out of thin air.

I laughed heartily. "My love! How is it that you seem to appear out of nowhere?"

My boy chuckled happily, his eyes crinkling at the corners. "I did a see-me-not spell, Rose. You are familiar with these?"

I nodded. It is a simple spell one does when wanting to mask oneself from another's eyes. I had never seen it done quite so convincingly. "Diarmuid," I said, loving the sound of his name.

"So, you've discovered me." He moved closer, chuckling and reaching out to me. I gave him my hand and was startled by a beautiful spark of magick. He led me down the path, toward my special altar. "I suppose you've also learned that I'm a not-to-be-trusted Leapvaughn."

"A Leapvaughn, aye, though I find you trustworthy." I lifted my chin to study his face. "You may be full of tricks, swinging from trees and juggling vegetables in the marketplace. But I find you to be honest."

"I believe you are wise beyond your years, Rose."

Under the cover of trees he pulled me into his arms, my body pressing against his. I had never known a man or boy in this way, feeling his legs and chest and hands upon me, enveloping me, inciting tiny wildfires beneath my skin.

Who could have imagined the power of love?

I had felt drawn to the Goddess on many occasions, but never had I felt this incredible desire to press into another person, to combine our two bodies in the simplest of unions.

He lowered his head, his soft lips meeting mine. I sucked in my breath and fell deep into his kiss, a sweet, languorous kiss. Then another, and another, and soon we were touching each other and performing a dance of kisses, soft, then severe, light, then dark and torturous. I wrapped my arms around his neck, gave myself over to him, and we tumbled onto a bed of moss, still kissing.

I don't know how long we danced that way—a chorus of moans and breathless sighs. When we fell apart and lay side by side, staring up at the Goddess's sky, our words seemed to shimmer like leaves in the summer breeze. I learned that he lived in

Lillipool, a Leapvaughn village several miles down the road. His father was a sheepherder, a job that Diarmuid hated. He preferred trade, which his father occasionally let him handle. He had been in Kirkloch trading sheep at auction the very day we met. He learned that my father had died when I was young, that I lived with my mother, who was the high priestess of our coven.

"I don't care that you're a Wodebayne," he said. "I wouldn't care if you were Ruanwande or Burnhyde or the daughter of a bestial dragon. I love you, Rose. As you are."

I dipped my hand into the opening of his shirt, pressing against his warm chest. "My friends cannot believe I have fallen into the arms of a Leapvaughn. Yet here I am, body and soul."

"We are mùirn beatha dàns," he whispered.

I nodded silently. Yes . . . my love knew it, too.

Two days—we'd had barely time to know each other. Yet I was utterly certain that he spoke the truth. We were soul mates. "So mote it be," I said.

"Aye, the Goddess has certainly brought us together." His fingers stroked the hair at the tender nape of my neck. "Who could imagine that She would bring me a tiny Wodebayne girl, with hair as black as a Samhain sky?"

" 'Tis an extraordinary match, to be sure. But the Goddess must have a purpose." I stared at the sky, watching as two fast-moving clouds raced into each other's path, melding into one. "Do you think we are to be the example to all clans? To prove that if the two of us, members of rival clans among many rivals, can come together in peace, so can all the clans?"

Diarmuid sat up and pulled my shoulders from the ground. "We are to be the champions of love. Our union will settle clan differences. End the age-old wars." He smiled proudly. "Could it be that the Goddess has chosen us for this noble task?"

"We will be the example of harmony under the Goddess's great blue sky." I leaned forward, brushing my cheek against his. "A noble task, yet hardly a task at all."

"Mmm . . ." His lips met mine for another deep kiss.

I melted against him, knowing it was true. We had been chosen. Ours would be an extraordinary love. The charm glowing at my breast was just the beginning of it all, thanks to the Goddess. I knew that we needed to pay homage to Her.

When the kiss ended, I arose and prepared a circle, sweeping it clean with my broom. Without wasting words, Diarmuid joined the cleansing ritual, working with me so naturally I felt as if we'd been raised in the same coven. He picked up two handfuls of dirt and spread them around the circle, moving so beautifully I nearly lost my way in the cleansing ritual.

Diarmuid turned to the east and stretched out his arms. "Ye Watchtowers of the East, I summon you, stir and call you, to witness this rite and watch over this circle." He waved his hand through the air, drawing something. A star? No, a pentagram.

I watched in wonder as he moved to the south quarter of the circle and beckoned the Watchtowers there. This was a practice I had never witnessed, and I wondered at the many things I might learn from him.

When he had called to the Watchtowers of the West and North, we ended up together in the center of the circle, facing the altar.

I lifted my hands to the moon. "The circle is cast, and we are between the worlds. We are far from the bonds of time, in a place where night and day, birth and death, joy and sorrow meet as one."

The forest seemed suddenly silent, our circle a haven of peace apart from the wars of the nearby clans and dreary villagers.

"O mighty Goddess, I have come this day to honor Your presence and to give thanksgiving for bringing Diarmuid to me. We who once were two will become one, Goddess, as we dedicate ourselves to You." I went to the altar and removed a pouch from my pocket. It was filled with dried sage, good for protection and wisdom. I poured the sage onto the altar, crushed it fine with a smooth stone, and pushed the tiny flakes onto the palm of my hand.

"We offer sage," I said, returning to Diarmuid's side. "Sage for protection against those who would harm us." I sprinkled the flaked herb over Diarmuid's head, then over my own. "Sage for the wisdom to fulfill the Goddess's will." I held my hand to his face, and he tipped back his head. I sprinkled sage onto his tongue, then poured the remainder into my own mouth. "Sage for protection and wisdom," I said, feeling a mist come over me.

"But you are wise already," Diarmuid said, taking my hands. He began to turn us in a circle. We moved slowly, but the earth seemed to race under our feet. "We have been chosen. The Goddess looks upon us with favor. How is it that She knows you so well?"

"I, Rose, am the Goddess incarnate," I answered. I was beyond thinking. Where had those words come from? Had I heard my mother chant them in an Esbat rite of long ago, or had the Goddess lifted my tongue like a winged bird at my back?

My whole world was spinning, my head dizzy with the whirring motion. Hands joined with Diarmuid, I lifted my face to the sky. It opened up upon me, sending a crushing blade of lightning to my chest.

The jolt lifted me off my feet. Suddenly my stomach was sour, my knees turning to mush beneath me. The ground seemed to rush up, sucking my body onto it.

The next thing I knew, my cheek was pressed to the earth, my knees curled beneath me like those of a child suckling its mother. My eyes were closed, but the whirring noise had stopped. The only sound was Diarmuid's voice calling my name.

"Rose? Are you all right?"

His hands were upon me, rubbing my shoulders, stroking my cheek.

"Aye." I sighed and sat up in his arms. "What happened? I've never been struck like that before."

"I don't know." Diarmuid pulled me closer into the cradle of his chest. "Are you sure you're not hurt?"

"Just . . . feeling in a haze." I brushed a lock of dark hair out of my eyes. I was stunned at the Goddess's sudden attack. Had I displeased Her? "I'm so confused. Why did that happen to me?"

"I've seen something like that, but only once. Our coven was gathered in a circle for Esbat rites, and the Goddess struck one of the witches down, very much like that. The coveners saw it as the hand of the Goddess reaching down, pointing to Her chosen one, her priestess. Soon after, the woman was anointed high priestess of our coven."

"High priestess . . ." I rubbed my eyes, still queasy from a churning inside me. "But I'm not in a coven looking for a leader."

"Ah, but the Goddess has chosen you," Diarmuid insisted. "I know that deep down inside me, Rose. You are destined for greatness. Have you not thought of inheriting your mother's role as high priestess?"

"Aye, but not for many years. Ma is not ready to relinquish her role, and she still sees me as a babe in the ways of the Goddess. She's always checking my Book of Spells and trying to pry into my rituals. Truly, she has no confidence in me."

"Well, on that she's mistaken." Diarmuid slid a hand around my waist, nearly knocking the air from me. "I'm sure you're destined to lead your own coven—or something even greater. You are special, Rose. Not just in my eyes, but in the eyes of the Goddess."

"I have to get home," I said, trying to rise. I coughed, and Diarmuid knelt beside me, then lifted me to my feet.

"Can you walk?" he asked. "For I can readily carry you there, such a wisp of a thing."

I tried a few steps. "I can make it. But I hate to go."

"I'll help you to the path," he said, lifting me into his arms.

I held fast to his shoulders, allowing myself a few moments of rest and protection in his arms. I had asked for protection, and the Goddess had answered already.

Diarmuid. He would be my pillar.

My soul mate.

5.
The Witch's Jar: A Spell of Protection

As darkness fell, the whirring pain within me began to settle, though the memory of it still frightened me. As Ma and I ate our stew thickened with the potatoes from Diarmuid, I noticed that she was still in a dour mood. I kept myself steady, not wanting to draw her ire upon me.

After I had cleaned the supper dishes, Ma brought out a clay jar to prepare for the spell of protection. "I don't believe you've ever done a witch's jar before, have you?"

I shook my head. "No, but I've collected many sharp objects. Just as you said." I opened the thick pouch and shook its contents onto the table with a tinny clatter.

"Fill the jar with everything you've found," Ma told me. "And as I remember, there are a few herbs that need to be added. Let me see." She took her Book of Shadows from its hiding place under the eaves of the cottage roof and set it on the table. "This is why I expect you to chronicle everything in your Book of Shadows, Rose. The mind does not always record as well as parchment and quill."

Another criticism. I dropped nails into the jar, wondering what I would have to do to please my mother in the ways of the Goddess.

My mother leafed through her book, her teeth pressed over her lower lip, until she found the right page. "Aye, we need sage and ivy," she said. "And a touch of bay should warn us of any further act of evil coming upon the MacGreavys." She ran her finger down the page, nodding. "And marjoram. Do we have that in our collection, Rose?"

"I think so." I got up from the table to check the pouches hanging from the rafters. "Aye, Ma, here it is." As I placed the pouch on the table, she caught my hand in hers.

Her touch sent a spark through me. Surprise, perhaps. Although I already knew I felt guilty for hiding so much from her.

"Something's changed, like shifting winds." She glanced up at me, her dark eyes locking on me. "Why do I have the feeling you're not telling me something, Rose? Are you all right?"

I nodded, trying to look away from her.

Ma rose to her feet, facing me. "What happened to you today? Did something go wrong in your ritual?"

I nodded again, too frightened of the painful experience to keep it pent up inside me. "I was . . . I was thanking the Goddess when She struck me down from the sky." I clasped my hands to my chest. "The force hit me here, knocking me to the ground. 'Twas like a lightning bolt on a sunny day and . . . oh, Ma, 'twas painful."

She folded me into her arms. "Child, child. Were you harmed?"

I closed my eyes and pressed my head to her blouse, relieved to have the truth out. "At first I could barely breathe, but I'm better now. Still frightened, though. Why would the Goddess strike me down?"

"'Tis hard to say." Ma stroked my hair, then moved me to a chair. "Have you done anything that might offend Her? Think hard, Rose, and be honest. What kind of spells have you been working on of late?"

I rubbed my forehead, wondering how to get through my web of lies without tripping over it. Surely my love spell for Diarmuid had not offended the Goddess so greatly? "Well, there was drawing down the moon. I did that with Kyra."

"'Tis not a spell, though."

"But we did work magick," I insisted. "We had a charm that needed to be charged."

"What sort of charm?"

As soon as she asked the question, I knew trouble was brewing for me. "It was a moonstone for Kyra," I said simply.

"And the purpose of the charm?"

"To bring her the love of Falkner Radburn."

"Oh, by the Goddess . . ." Ma banged her fist on the table, making the witch's jar jump a bit. "How many times have I told you not to meddle with a person's free will? You can make a charm or a poppet to attract love, but it's wrong to ensnare the love of a specific person. To meddle with a person's life, to control his destiny . . . that's dark magick." She banged her fist again. "It's wrong, Rose!"

My insides turned stone cold at her anger. Couldn't she see I was just helping a very desperate friend?

"Why is it that all my instructions to you fly through the air and fall to the soil?" my mother asked. "You are not listening, Rose, and today is just one example of how the power of the Goddess can harm if you don't practice witchcraft in the ways of the elders. Do you want to hurt people, Rose?"

"No, Ma," I said quietly. That much was true.

"Then why do you insist on meddling with a person's will? 'Tis not right, Rose. When you go out to gather plants, do you strike down a plant without apology? Do you slash through stems at will, taking more than you need, harming nature?"

"No." I dug my fingers into my hair, dropping my chin against my chest. I hated being chastised this way. I thought of Diarmuid's comment that he had seen a woman struck down the same way because she was destined to be the high priestess of the coven. Why could my ma not even entertain the thought that there was a positive reason? Could it be that she knew I had been chosen by the Goddess for greatness, and she was jealous of my connection to Her? My face burned at the thought.

"So why would you strike out at a person that way, tampering with his destiny?"

There was no answer—at least, none that would suit her—so I kept quiet.

"You must go back to your earlier lessons," Ma said sternly. "Starting tomorrow, you will look over your Book of Shadows from the beginning. You will spend less time afield with your friends and more time studying from my Book of Shadows, too. And you will stop making up your own spells until I can be sure you're fulfilling the Goddess's will. Do you understand?"

"I understand," I said. I pressed my teeth into my lower lip, wondering if she would realize that I had not promised her anything.

It was all so unfair. I had tried to gain my mother's support by telling her about the painful strike from the sky, and in turn she merely wanted to cripple me. If Síle the high priestess had her way, I'd be locked in the cottage, drying herbs and inscribing spells.

How could I stop making spells when I knew the Goddess was calling me to Her? How dare my mother try to interfere with the Goddess's destiny for me?

Ma did not understand about my powers. And from her tart reaction on that front, I knew that it would be a catastrophe to tell her about Diarmuid.

For now he would be a secret, and until my mother learned to see me as more than her incapable daughter, he would remain a secret.

Down the dark road, Miller MacGreavy led the way. He was followed by his wife, who walked beside my mother, their voices lowered so as not to wake anyone in the cottages we passed. I walked behind them, feeling dull and tired. The night's Esbat rites had hardly moved me. They had only emphasized how Síle and her coven were following a weary, timeworn road while I was on the verge of opening an exciting new doorway to the Goddess.

The breeze rustled the trees so ripe with bud; their clattering branches reminded me of the bell rung at Esbat.

Three times.

"An ye harm none, do what thou wilt," Síle chanted.

"An ye harm none, do what thou wilt," we all repeated.

"Thus runs the Witch's Rede," Síle went on. "Remember it well. Whatever you desire; whatever you would ask of the Goddess, be assured that it will harm no one—not even yourself. And remember that as you give, so it shall return threefold."

I trudged along, trying to clear my mother's voice from my

head. I had heard her words in the circle so many times, I could recite them by heart.

"I am She who watches over thee," said High Priestess Síle. "Mother of you all. Know that I rejoice that you do not forget me, paying me homage at the full of the moon. Know that I weave the skein of life for each and every one of you. . . ."

"Enough, enough, enough!" I grumbled through gritted teeth. I had heard my mother's words so many times, they had become meaningless for me.

As we neared the mill, I wondered if Ma's spell of protection would work. At least this was something that interested me, as I'd never worked one before. Miller MacGreavy unlatched the big door to the mill, and the four of us filed inside. During the Esbat rites, Ma and the MacGreavys had summoned the Goddess to protect them and the mill, so I imagined that this would entail more spell casting than the ritual had.

Soon Ma had candles lit, and Mrs. MacGreavy set her tools on the table, which we assembled around. Normally I would have helped with preparations, but since Ma had made it clear I was being punished, I held back. Ma had already placed herbs in the witch's jar, which now sat at the center of the table, but I knew there was something more to be added before we sealed it.

Closing her eyes, Ma held up her hands, opened to the Goddess. "With this witch's jar we will cast a spell of protection over this mill and this miller's family," she said. Looking down at the table, she moved the jar toward Mrs. MacGreavy. "'Twill need a drop of blood from you. Take your bolline and give your finger the slightest prick."

The miller's wife pressed the sharp end of her bolline

against her fingertip. A crimson drop began to form, and she squeezed it into the jar.

Then my mother passed the jar over to the miller. "Spit in it," she said. He did so. Then Ma began to seal the top of the jar, using hot candle wax. As she worked, she chanted:

> "Protect this mill, protect these folk,
> Guard them from illness and harm.
> Send back the darkness to those who sent it.
> Cast a light of goodness around,
> Let love and protection abound."

Glancing up from the sealed jar, my mother told the MacGreavys to join hands. "You must remain here in the mill while Rose and I circle it with the jar. Three times." She pulled on her cloak and went to the door. "We'll be back when the spell is finished."

Silently I followed my mother. I was allowed to hold the jar as we traced a wide circle around the mill. On the side where the brook ran deep and fast, there was a crossing bridge. But as we reached the shallows on the other side of the mill, it was clear there was no way across.

"No way across but in," Ma said, gathering up her skirts. "Pull up your gown, Rose. We'll be walking through the Goddess's waters tonight." She stuck out her foot, eyeing her sandal. "Too bad it's not a cobbler we're casting a spell for. We'll be in need of new footwear after this."

I laughed, taken aback at Ma's impetuous humor. This was a side of her I rarely saw. I hitched up my skirts and stepped into the brook. Cold water swirled around my legs and mud seeped into my shoes, but I tramped on beside Ma, the witch's jar tucked into the crook of my arm.

We circled the mill three times, then ducked inside with sodden shoes and wet legs. The cold didn't bother me. It was sort of refreshing on a warm night, and I counted this spell as something of value, certainly worth including in my Book of Shadows.

Inside the mill, the MacGreavys waited in the flickering candlelight.

"The spell is done," Ma said. "We need to bury the jar, but there's no safe place around here. Rose and I will hide it in the woods where no one will find it."

The miller went over to my mother, clasping her hands. "Thank you, Síle."

She nodded. "And now I think I need a rag to wipe down my shoes. Seems that Rose and I had to go for a late night dip in the brook." She pushed off her shoe, and it flopped onto the floor like a dead fish.

"Oh, my!" Mrs. MacGreavy laughed, rushing off to find some cloths.

The miller brought out chairs and wine for all of us, and he and his wife talked in the quiet, dark room while Ma and I dried our feet. I took a sip of wine—sweet and heady. Just like Diarmuid's kisses. Of course, nearly everything made me think of Diarmuid. It was an effort to concentrate on what was before me instead of the lovely picture floating in my mind of him. And at the moment, the conversation was so gloomy, with the miller complaining of slow business, that I preferred to dream of my love.

"At least it was our slow season," Mrs. MacGreavy was saying.

"Aye, but if we don't get that broken gear fixed soon, we'll have no business at all," Miller MacGreavy said. "It's all a result of the curse upon us, probably from those vile Burnhydes." He turned to Ma. "And I thank you for wiping it away. Our luck will change now, though I can't say that I see better days ahead for the Seven Clans. It's an age-old battle we're fighting, and it's getting worse instead of better, with curses and sheep thieves and vendors picking on innocent young girls at market." His eyes burned with conviction as he glanced at me, and I bit my lower lip, wondering if everyone in the Highlands had heard of my escapades at the market. If the story was floating around, soon the real details—of the boy who had saved me—would wend their way to my mother. More trouble for me.

"Ian . . ." The miller's wife tried to soothe him, but he forged on.

"I say it's high time we Wodebaynes stopped taking the prejudice against us," he insisted. "Time to use magick to fight back."

Closing her eyes, my mother shook her head gently. "No, Ian, that's not the answer."

"Well, then, how are we going to stop it, Síle?" the miller asked. "You know the stories—though there are so many, I've lost count. A Leapvaughn tricking a Wodebayne farmer out of his land. A Ruanwande casting a spell that makes a Wodebayne girl go mad. Even your own husband, Gowan, was prey to the prejudice, Síle."

"My father?" I dropped the rag on the floor. So long had I craved to hear stories of my father, Gowan MacEwan, but every time I asked, my request was headed off by a severe look from my mother. "Tell me," I begged, turning to the man.

"'Tis not much of a story, Rose," the miller said, touching his beard. "But one day, when your father was on the road traveling to a nearby village, he came across a Wyndonkylle man on a horse. The horseman rode past without incident but then returned to harass your father. He accused your father of looking upon him with evil in his eyes. Then, when he learned that your father was a Wodebayne, he reared up his horse and trampled your father under its hooves."

I winced. "That's a terrible tale. But Da survived it."

Ma nodded. "Aye, but he walked with a limp ever after."

As Mr. MacGreavy went on lamenting the clan differences, I thought of my father. He had died when I was young, so I remembered little of him. I'd heard a few dark rumors—tales that he had been interested in dark magick—though no one spoke of him to me directly. And my mother refused to fill in any of the missing details. Why was she so reluctant to speak of him?

After the conversation and wine ran out, we said our good-byes and headed home. Ma and I were across the river and down the road a bit when she realized we had forgotten the witch's jar.

"Make haste and fetch it," she told me. "I shall wait here."

Lifting my skirts, I ran back along the road. But as I approached the mill, I saw a solitary candle burning upon the threshold. I slowed my pace as my feet silently crept over the cooling earth. There was magick here—I felt the boundaries of a witch's circle, and I was forced to stop at its perimeters. I used my magesight to study the details. Was that a pentagram drawn in the dirt by the door? But it was upside down! 'Twas not part of the spell Ma had cast. . . .

As I stood in the shadows, a figure loomed in the open doorway—Miller MacGreavy. He did not sense my presence as he leaned out and poured a dark liquid over the pentagram, all the while uttering words I did not understand. I gasped, realizing that the liquid Ian MacGreavy was using was blood.

The very tone of the scene made me shudder. 'Twas as if a cold wind had swept up the river, turning everything in its path to ice.

Dark magick. I gasped.

Miller MacGreavy twitched in fear, darting a look toward me. "Rose?" he asked suspiciously. "What are you doing here?"

"The witch's jar," I croaked in fear. "We . . . we left it behind."

He scowled at me, then ducked back inside. A moment later he reappeared with the jar, stepping around the pentagram and drawing a door in his circle to step out toward me.

His eyes glittered in the candlelight as he handed me the jar. "Begone with you, Rose MacEwan," he said angrily. "And not a word to anyone of what you witnessed here tonight."

"Aye, sir," I said breathlessly. Although I feared his magick, I knew it was not cast against me. Still, his warning frightened me. Best to keep it to myself. After all, it appeared he wasn't harming an innocent.

Yet even as I tucked away my memory of Miller MacGreavy, I decided not to let the matter of my father rest. On the way home from the mill that night I waited until my heartbeat slowed to a more relaxed pace, then launched into the subject. "I was glad to hear the story of Da," I said, walking slowly under the orange moonlight. "We set a place for him every year at the Samhain table, yet you never tell me stories about him. You never speak of him, Ma. Why is that?"

My mother took a deep breath, searching for the answer. "It always pained me to speak of him. The way his life was snuffed out . . . the way it ended. It was a terrible thing, Rose." She linked her arm through mine. "I supposed I thought that if we didn't talk about it, you might be spared the pain that I felt."

I shook my head. "When I think of him, there's no pain, really. Just curiosity."

"What do you remember of him?"

Thinking of Da, I smiled. "His largeness. He was a bear of a man, was he not?"

"Quite large," Ma agreed.

"I remember riding on his shoulders—big, broad shoulders. And his hands. They were so huge, my little hand disappeared inside his. I remember his deep, ringing laugh. And a trip to the coast. Did he take me to the seacoast?"

My mother nodded.

"I've heard the rumors of him," I said. "That he subscribed to dark magic. Is that true, Ma?"

"No," she said gently. "I'll never believe that. He was a good man; he loved his family, his child, his clan. He was simply misunderstood."

Like me, I thought. Ma didn't understand my powers or my adventurous spirit. She couldn't accept that her path to the Goddess was not the only way.

"I wish you'd had a chance to know him well," my mother said.

We walked for a few moments, then I asked, "What of his death? Did he not die in his sleep?"

"He did."

"Then what of all the rumors? That he was cursed—or poisoned by a rival clan?"

"That is the most difficult part," my mother admitted. "His death was suspicious. Sudden and unexplainable. Some say a rival clan cursed him in retaliation; I don't know."

"Retaliation for what?"

Ma shook her head and her mouth grew tight. "I cannot speak of matters that I know nothing of." When she turned to me, tears glimmered in her eyes. "And I tell you truly, Rose, I do not know the truth of his death."

She fell silent, but that silence haunted me as we walked on. Aye, Ma might not have understood Da's death, but certainly she knew more of the details than I. As usual, she wasn't giving me enough pieces to patch the thing together in my mind.

I thought of Ian MacGreavy, of the way his body had loomed over the bloody pentagram. Had my father dabbled with taibhs, too? I cast my eyes to the distant moon, wondering. . . .

The next day, after hiding the witch's jar in a deserted thicket, I met Diarmuid at our secret place in the woods. On this day we wasted no time with small talk or teasing. He pulled me into his arms and placed his lips on mine. The kiss stole my breath away, and we tumbled onto the green moss and lay there, kissing and holding and stroking each other until the sun ventured below the treetops.

He told me that the magick in his own Esbat circle had paled in comparison to what we had done together.

"Aye," I told him, "I felt the same way last night." I went over to my small, makeshift altar and smoothed my hands over the surface of the boulder. Looking around, I realized that this was the perfect place for a circle—our circle.

I grabbed my broom and with measured steps walked farther than I had before. I would make the circle wider, this time including the moss bed we liked to frolic upon. Was not our love dedicated to the Goddess—a result of her blessings?

Diarmuid went to the four corners of the new, bigger circle, where he summoned the Watchtowers once again, drawing a pentagram in the air each time. Watching Diarmuid, I felt my world swelling with newfound knowledge and love. The rose stone between my breasts set my heart aglow, reminding me of my good fortune at having found a true love who was also a blood witch.

The day after that we met again, same time, same place. And the day after that and the day after that. My spring afternoons were lush affairs of lips trailing on skin and countless whispered dreams under the cool cover of spring leaves. Each day we maintained our altar, always thanking the Goddess for bringing us together, for bringing us so much pleasure.

"Our destiny is not clear to me yet," I once told Diarmuid. "But I know there's a reason we've been brought together."

He dipped his face into the bodice of my gown, nuzzling there seductively. "'Tis not enough that we were brought together to love?"

"Love is a gift, indeed," I said, slipping my hands into the top of his shirt to find his gold pentagram. "But I'm talking about a greater purpose. Bringing the Seven Clans together, perhaps."

He moved up to kiss my neck. "Our love is truly beyond all others." He stopped kissing me to look me in the eye. "I've known people who say they are mùirn beatha dàns. They truly believe they are soul mates for life. But I can't imagine that they would understand the way I feel about you."

He smoothed his hand over my bodice, cupping one breast gently. "I love you, Rose."

I gasped, feeling myself melt at his fingertips. I had never known a man before, and Diarmuid swore I was his first love, yet he seemed more experienced than I was.

"We'll be together forever," he whispered.

"We'll have no secrets," I vowed.

"I shall be your first and only love," he said. "And you shall be mine."

"So mote it be," I whispered, offering our love to the Goddess.

There, in our secret circle in the woods, we met every afternoon. One day as Diarmuid and I lay together on the moss, I realized that we had been together for nearly a full cycle of the moon. The May celebration of Beltane was but a few weeks away, and Diarmuid and I had met just before the full moon of April.

I thought of the two charmed gemstones that had been the seeds of love: the rose stone and Kyra's moonstone. Two charms with very different powers.

Oh, Kyra and Falkner were still together and very much in love. But not like Diarmuid and me. Just that morning I had seen Kyra at Sunday mass, and she had been full of giggles and squeals for her boy. Like a child. She knew that I met Diarmuid each day, and she couldn't believe I'd allowed him a kiss, let alone other pleasures.

"But what do you do with Falkner?" I asked.

"I bring him biscuits and shortbread every time Ma and I bake," she said. "And he stops by the cottage if he has to deliver a newly shod horse nearby. Which isn't often. So sometimes Ma allows me to accompany her to market in Kirkloch and we stop in at the blacksmith's shop."

"Oh." I didn't tell her that it all sounded tedious and lack-luster to me. If it suited Kyra, that was fine. But hearing about her love for Falkner made me realize the level of maturity Diarmuid and I had reached. We were far beyond blushes and giggles. Our love had ventured into passion, promise . . .

And commitment.

"Come back to me, my love," Diarmuid said, pulling me onto my side. "You've wandered so far into the clouds, I'd dare not venture to guess your thoughts."

"Ah, but I'm here," I said, "thinking of you."

As Beltane approached and preparations began, it became more and more difficult for Diarmuid and me to steal away for our afternoon meetings. One day he was late, and I worried the time away, despairing that I would not see him at all. I was about to leave when I received a tua labra from Diarmuid, a silent message that only witches can send: *Wait for me, my love.* I waited, and within moments he was dashing into my arms, apologizing and explaining about the tedious chores his father had given him that day. Another day Ma seemed more suspicious than usual, and I had to concoct a preposterous lie to sneak off to his arms.

"The strain of saying good-bye to you each afternoon is wearing on me," I told him as we sat in the moss.

"Aye, and each time it's without knowing that we'll both make it back." He sucked in a deep breath. "It's getting more and more difficult for us to be together, Rose. Your ma is suspicious, and my da keeps loading me up with work."

"I know it, and I thought the Goddess would ease our burdens." He lifted his hand to my cheek, and I pressed against him longingly.

"Blast them all, we should tell them! Let them know of our love!"

His brash spirit made my heart soar. "Would you?" I said. "And would that be an act of courage or foolishness? For no one is ready to learn of us yet. They would either try to tear us apart—or banish us from our clans!"

Diarmuid's blue eyes clouded with concern. "You're right. And I will protect you, Rose. I won't have you ostracized by Leapvaughns or Wodebaynes or anyone."

"We must go forth with caution," I said. I knew the Goddess had deigned that we be together, but how could we begin to clear the way with the rest of the world?

As Diarmuid stroked my hair gently, the answer came upon me.

Make final the bond.

"The Goddess wants us to be together," I said. "Heart, spirit . . . and body." Grabbing Diarmuid's shirt, I pulled him closer. "We must seal our love with a physical union."

His eyes sparkled with wonder. "'Tis the Goddess's will?"

"Aye." I nodded, thinking of the upcoming celebration. There would be maypole ribbons fluttering in the breeze, flowers and songs and the scent of burning sage. Each covener would take a ribbon and dance around the maypole, symbolizing the union of man and woman, the joining of all together. "And Beltane will be the perfect time."

6.
Night Visions

Tiny fingers.

I have short, pudgy fingers, and my da has the hands of a giant. Sometimes he holds me in his palm and lifts me in the air, allowing me to see the world the way birds and flies do. Other times, like now, I ride on his shoulders, laughing because he is reaching up to tickle me behind the knees.

We are at the seashore. The grass is so green here, and from the high cliffs you can see miles and miles of emerald field and roiling teal waters. Da hikes along the cliffside with me upon his shoulders. Occasionally the ocean rises up and smashes against the rocky cliff with a fierce temper, but we laugh at it. My da even dances closer, trying to catch the spray. Tiny droplets of water drench us, but we rejoice.

Da turns so suddenly that I am nearly wrenched out of his arms. I look to see what has alarmed him, and there it is, rising up like a dragon. The ocean is rising, higher and higher in a ferocious wave.

And then, when I look again, my da is not there. Only his laughter remains—a hollow, mean sound as the giant wave looms over me. Its monstrous tendrils rise, its power surging overhead.

I am alone on the cliff, a wave curling over me.

I try to run, but my tiny legs are weak, like the twig legs of a marionette. There is really no escape . . . yet escape is everything.

Somehow I know there is much to be lost if I succumb to the wave. It's not only my life at stake, but also the lives and futures of all my clan, all the Wodebaynes, as well as the Braytindales and Leapvaughns and the witches of all Seven Clans.

So much at stake, but how can I escape?

How to get away from the ominous wave closing over my head?

"Rose? Rose! You must awaken."

Gasping for breath, I tried to pull myself from sleep and navigate safely to the sound of my mother's voice.

"Rose, child, you've had a night vision."

I felt her hands on my arms, shaking me gently. Opening my eyes, I realized that I was in the cottage, safe and dry. But fear held me in its grip, and I was unable to shake it.

"It's all right, child," Ma said. "Tell me what you saw."

I squeezed my eyes shut, afraid to talk about it. Afraid to open up to the woman I'd lied to so much of late. I had guarded my feelings and fears from Ma. How could I open up to her now?

She rubbed my back gently but firmly, up and down between my shoulders. A soothing warmth went through me, reminding me of all the times Ma had rubbed my back when I was sick or frightened or frustrated at not being able to master something. Whether it was the emotion of the dream or the tenderness of Ma's gesture, I wasn't sure. But suddenly I was crying.

"I was at the coast with Da," I said, spilling out the details of my dream. I told Ma everything . . . about my father leaving me and about the giant wave that had been about to slam into me. "I don't understand it. Please, Ma, please tell me the truth," I said. "Was Da an evil man? Did he ever try to hurt me?"

"Oh, no, child!" Ma insisted. "Gowan MacEwan loved you dearly. The man did everything in his power to protect us."

"Then why did he leave me behind in the dream, Ma? What does it mean?"

My mother pursed her lips thoughtfully. In the dim moonlight seeping in through the window she looked old, with lines creasing the corners of her mouth. "Perhaps he left you in the dream because he left you so early in life," she said. "Or perhaps the rumors of his death make you suspicious of him."

"Did he really die in his sleep, here in the cottage?"

"Aye." She sighed, and I felt sure she would change the subject as usual. "'Twas so sudden, his death," she murmured, as if to herself. "All the coveners suspected that someone had cast a dark spell upon him. Many said that the threefold law of magick was the reason for his death."

I thought about the threefold law—that magick returns to the sender magnified three times. In this way dark magick would hurt the sender the most. "But that would mean that he was practicing dark magick, that he had fallen away from the ways of the Goddess."

"Aye," Ma agreed, staring off into the distance, "and I'll never believe that of your father." She stood up from my bedside and beckoned me to follow. "Come. Let's cleanse the cottage for sweet dreams."

While Ma lit the candles, I swept the center of the cottage to create a small circle around our table. I was surprised to see that she had taken out our yellow candles, which were usually reserved for special occasions, but she explained that they were to help me gain true vision. "It's time you learned to have a second sight, to see past the ordinary and witness the Goddess's will."

I swallowed hard in amazement. How was it that she knew of my own plan? At that moment I wanted to sit down and tell her everything about Diarmuid, but as she started chanting over the candles, something held me back. Standing in the lemon circle of light, I watched as Ma beseeched the Goddess to bring me vision, to show me Her will for me.

Then Ma brought me to the center of the circle, and, standing behind me, she wrapped her arms around me. I felt so loved and protected there in her arms—like a child again.

"Gracious Goddess," she said, "let Your love rain down upon Rose. Show her the path she must pursue to fulfill her destiny. Walk with her through this time of darkness to come again into the light."

"So mote it be," I said.

My mother's hands went to my head. She stroked my hair back gently, then clasped her hands around my skull. "Rid her mind of frightening night visions. Let her see only Your vision, Goddess. Rid both our minds of dark thoughts. Chase evil from our home."

"So mote it be," I repeated as a warm feeling came over me. Leaning back against Ma, I remembered how she had summoned the Goddess to help me when I was little—to cool a feverish head, to guard me against eating a poisonous herb, to give me the wisdom to learn my runes. Ma and I had been at odds so much of late, but I knew that despite all of her disapproval and criticism, she did love me, her only daughter.

And in time, she would come to love Diarmuid as a son.

7.

Beltane Rites, the Fifth Day of May

"Spring daisies and cornflowers," Kyra said, climbing over some flat rocks to reach another patch of wildflowers. "With the early spring we've had this year, 'twill be one of the most colorful Beltane rites ever."

As was our annual practice, Kyra and I had risen before dawn to creep into the woods on a quest for flowers. We would hang fresh flowers on the doors of our cottages and strew them about the circle in gay decoration for the night's festivities. We would also make a crown of fresh flowers to be worn by the high priestess. Today I would make an extra crown—one for myself.

"I think Beltane is my favorite celebration of the year," I said. "And this year 'twill be my most memorable." I silently thanked the lilac bush for her offering, then used my bolline to cut off a fat bunch of fragrant flowers.

"Because you are in love?" Kyra asked.

I pressed the lavender blooms to my cheek. "Because I shall become a woman in love, in every rite." When Kyra's brows lifted in curiosity, I explained, "Diarmuid and I shall have our own maypole celebration tonight. Do you see the ribbons I took from the cottage?" I reached into my pocket and pulled out streamers of red and white ribbons.

"What?" Kyra's mouth dropped open.

"Aye, red and white ribbons to signify the blood that flows from a woman when her purity is taken. For that's how Diarmuid and I will celebrate Beltane."

"This I cannot believe!" Kyra screeched. "Do you know what you're doing, Rose?"

"Aye." I twirled around in the field, letting the ribbons stream behind me. "I know quite well. I believe the Goddess has called us together for this. And Beltane is a festival of love and union, is it not?"

Kyra swallowed hard. "I don't know that the Goddess intends us to take every detail so literally."

I danced over to Kyra and tugged on her hand. "Don't be an old toad in the mire! We're seventeen years under the Goddess's sky."

"Aye, but there's been no handfasting, no joining of the two of you in the circle."

"That will come later," I insisted, pulling her into my dance.

She dropped her basket and spun around with me, our eyes meeting in laughter until we grew dizzy and dropped to the grass.

"Oh, dear Goddess, now You've convinced me," Kyra said, staring up into the clear blue sky. "Rose has lost her wits."

"I have not!" I protested. "And I'll wager that you'll be telling me the same thing soon, about you and Falkner."

"I can't imagine it, though I am so in love."

I rolled onto my side and squeezed her arm. "You must pretend that I'm with you, tonight after the circle."

"Oh, Rose, you know I am a terrible teller of tales."

"'Twill be nothing. The younger coveners always end up celebrating a bit on their own as the others dance by the light of the Beltane fires. Just tell Ma I am with you."

"Lying to the high priestess," she said. "Goddess, forgive me."

"I knew I could rely on you." I stood up and brushed grass from my hair. "We'd best go and see to the decorations."

We filled our baskets until they were brimming over with blossoms, then headed back to our cottage. Ma looked on as we made bunches to hang on the doors, leaving aside other flowers to decorate the circle. Then Ma set some sage leaves afire in a clay pot, and we blew off the flames until the burning ashes produced a pungent smoke, which we spread through the cottage.

As we set about our tasks, Kyra spoke of Falkner, how he thought her the best baker in the Highlands, how he had come to visit her just the day before. Ma did not comment until we were finished smoking the house and ready to head over and do the same to Kyra's cottage. That was when she brought out the sewing basket along with a few old snatches of cloth.

"Hearing you talk of young Falkner, I've come to think you should put your thoughts into action," Ma told Kyra. "If you truly want to bring love into your life, it's wrong to trap a particular person, as you did with the charmed moonstone."

Kyra lowered her head. "I'm sorry, ma'am. I know."

"Trapping a person with a spell is dark magick," Síle said. "It has the potential to harm someone by tinkering with their destiny and stripping away their free will. However," Ma went on, "the Goddess can help you bring love into your life, as long as you're not targeting a particular person and meddling with their destiny. You can work love magick through poppets." She placed two pieces of cloth together and began to cut. As she trimmed away the cloth, the shape of a gingerbread man began to emerge. "You must make two small dolls—one to represent you, the other to represent the boy, or man, of your dreams."

I watched carefully as Ma showed us how to make the poppets. She helped Kyra sew brown ribbon on the girl doll to make it resemble herself.

Then Ma handed Kyra the boy doll to decorate. "Make him handsome in your eyes, but don't inscribe him with a name or a rune that points to a particular person."

Kyra thanked Ma when we finished, then we raced off to decorate her cottage and our coven's meeting place in the woods. It was afternoon when our work was done. Kyra headed home to bake some of the ceremonial cakes with her ma, and I headed off to decorate my own maypole. We were just about to go our separate ways, when a tall chestnut horse came trotting up the road. It was a majestic sight, the rider sitting tall.

"It's Falkner," Kyra said, patting down her hair.

"'Tis not," I muttered, blinking into the sunlight. Kyra was right, though I had not expected this beanpole of a boy to be transformed into a knight.

"Good day!" Kyra called, waving wildly.

Falkner stopped his horse as it reached us, then swept down and landed at Kyra's feet. "Would you like a ride?" he offered Kyra and me. "I've got to return the horse. Da just fixed his shoes, but you may ride along the way."

"I'm headed off into the woods," I said, "but Kyra has been afoot all day, preparing for tonight."

"Are you tired, then?" he asked her, the fondness in his eyes unmistakable.

She nodded at him sweetly, and he boosted her up onto the horse's back. "There you go."

"Thank you." Gazing down at him, Kyra seemed like a different person. Not the gawky braided girl who used to skip over stones in the brook, but . . . a woman.

The image stayed in my head as we parted ways. On my way through the woods I stopped by the brook and sat down at the water's edge. Here the water slowed into a clear, still pool, where tiny minnows darted through the weeds and bugs skittered along the glassy surface. I reached down to cup a drink of water but stopped, startled. Staring back at me was the face of the Goddess.

No, 'twas but a reflection of a woman. Me.

I had grown in the ways of the Goddess, and I was ready to take the next step. For Beltane was not only a feast of love, it was a feast of fertility. It was a time for joining two halves to make a whole—the third entity. And although every young witch knew the spell to cast to close the door to the womb, I would not speak that spell. My lunar bleeding was but a week's past.

I was ready to have his child.

Laughter rumbled through the forest as the coven's Beltane celebration wound down. Sitting on a log, Kyra's father strummed a lute and another covener piped, making merry music for revelers to enjoy. In another part of the circle I sat with the young coveners, finishing up the last of the cakes and wine.

"There you are," Falkner said to Kyra, who giggled behind her hand. "I tell you, it looks quite fine that way, unbridled and untethered." He had removed one of the braids from her hair and was now combing through it intimately with his fingers.

Kyra pressed a fat flower into his face. "You are such a silly goose," she teased.

As far as I was concerned, they were both quite silly, but perhaps I was just impatient to be off to my own Beltane cele-bration. And worried. What if Ma would not let me go? What if Diarmuid could not get away?

"'Tis time to leave the circle to the elders," I told the oth-ers around me. Kyra agreed, and plans were made to head off to Falkner's cottage. I crossed my fingers as we went to our parents for approval, but the festive, relaxed mood prevailed. "Just beware that you are not spotted traveling in a group," my mother advised us. "'Tis a night to revel, but we must not let the Christians get wind of our celebration."

I could hear my mother laughing with friends as we left the circle. Within minutes we were a distance away, and I was saying good-bye to Kyra.

"Be careful!" she whispered before Falkner pulled her away with the others.

I just smiled as I walked quickly through the dark night.

Diarmuid's dark figure was unmistakable. Standing naked under the maypole tree, he was silhouetted by the small fire he had lit in the north quarter of the circle. Now my eyes feasted on what my hands had explored, his rounded muscles, long limbs, smooth skin. He was a god. The red and white ribbons fluttered in the air over his head; the same wind feathered the hair from his noble forehead. The night was dark, the new moon having just passed, but Diarmuid's skin seemed to glow from across the clearing as I paused.

The space between us seemed alive with warmth. Around us the forest sang, its crickets and toads and swaying trees a symphony so clear and sweet, even a deaf man could hear its answer.

I loosened the girdle at my waist, then dropped my own gown to the ground so that I was wearing only a shift. The rustle of cloth made him turn my way, and he smiled. I ran across the clearing and Diarmuid caught me in his arms against his warm body. We were meant to be together, to participate in this rite tonight. I noticed that he had already lit the candles, so I swept the circle while he called upon the four Watchtowers, drawing pentagrams in the air. Then we went to the maypole and each took a ribbon.

"'Tis a time for joy and a time for sharing," I said as I started to walk around the tree. "The richness of the soil accepts the seeds. For now is the time that seed should be spilled." I knew the words to most Greater Sabbats by heart, but today this particular ritual seemed so fitting! "Let us celebrate the planting of abundance," I went on. "The turning of the Wheel, the season of the Goddess. Let us say farewell to the darkness and greet the light."

"The Wheel turns," Diarmuid said. He walked behind me, wrapping his ribbon over mine.

"Without ceasing, the Wheel turns."

"And turns again," he said as our ribbons twined as inexorably as our love.

When the tree was wrapped with a lovely weave of red and white, we went to the altar, where the crown of early red roses and daisies lay. Diarmuid lifted off my shift, then picked up the crown and held it over my head.

"The Goddess has brought us through the darkness to the light," he said. He lowered the crown to my head, and I felt the heady fragrance of the roses surround me. "Now our Goddess is among us," Diarmuid whispered, his eyes sparkling. "Speak, Lady."

"I am the one who turns the Wheel," I said evenly. I felt the pulse of the Goddess within me, steady and strong, hungry and ravenous. My body was ready to take on his seed, my spirit prepared to mingle with his. "When you thirst," I said, "let my tears fall upon you as gentle rain. When you tire, pause to rest upon the earth that is my breast. Know that love is the spark of life, the fire within you. Love is the beginning and the end of all things."

I opened my arms to Diarmuid, the light of the fire dancing over my body. "And I am love," I whispered.

The next morning I left my bed at dawn to bathe in the spring. Most days I simply wash with a rag, but today I went to the deep part of the brook for a more thorough cleansing.

On the grassy bank I glanced around to make sure no one else was afoot. A peahen rushed through the bushes, but otherwise the woods were quiet. Quickly I slipped out of my robe and stepped into the brook. The water was cold, barely two lunar cycles away from the last winter snow, but I ventured all the way in, submerging myself to my neck, just below where my hair was knotted.

A cleansing.

And an offering.

I touched my belly, wondering at the tiny babe inside me. I had a new life to offer up to the Goddess—Diarmuid's baby. Already I knew it to be true, but my secret would grow safe within my belly for a few months. There would be enough time to work on our two clans, time to help them accept Diarmuid and me as man and wife.

Waving my arms through the water, I smiled. My whole body felt aglow with the promise of motherhood. This child would tie us together in a physical way. I knew our baby was another part of the Goddess's plan, which was slowly being revealed to us. I was eager to tell Diarmuid, but for now I would keep my secret as a delightful surprise to be enjoyed after our love was sanctioned by the clans.

Feeling cleansed and refreshed, I arose from the waters and climbed onto the muddy bank. Quickly I pulled on my robe and stepped into my sandals.

But what was that noise?

I peered out of the bushes, searching the path. There was no one in sight, though I felt a strong sense of another's presence.

Had someone been watching me?

8.
Esbat Rites, Mid-July

"When the moon is full and the sky is dark,
We meet within our circle.
Now hear the singing of the lark
And dance in the circle, move in the circle.
Do what thou wilt if it harms none,
As the Goddess wills it, may it be done."

A covener sang as we stood in the coven circle, surrounding the High Priestess Síle. Falkner played a pipe, and Kyra joined in the music by beating on small drum. I think she and Falkner had devised the ruse of practicing their music in order to spend time together—as if their parents weren't wise to their swelling emotions. Kyra had mentioned something of it, but I had been so wrapped up in attempting to see Diarmuid that I'd lost track of the details.

The music ended, and Síle called two coveners—Kyra's parents—to come forward for the cake and wine ceremony. Side by side, Lyndon and Paige stepped before the altar, where Ma handed Paige a goblet of wine.

Paige lifted the goblet with both hands and held it between her breasts. Facing her, Lyndon took his athame and held the handle between his two palms, the blade pointing down.

Slowly he dipped his blade into the wine, saying: "In like fashion may male join female for the happiness of both."

"Let the fruits of union promote life," Paige responded. "Let all be fruitful and let prosperity spread throughout the land."

Lyndon raised his athame, and his wife held the goblet to his lips so that he could drink. When he finished, he held the goblet for her affectionately.

Watching them, I felt a stirring inside me. Could it be my child waking lazily? My belly had not begun to grow yet, but I had noticed a heaviness in my breasts. Diarmuid had noticed, too, and had teased me that I was coming into womanhood. I still had not told him, and he did not yet realize that my body was preparing to nurse a child. Glancing around the circle, my eyes fixed upon Kyra, whose face was alight tonight, probably warmed by her love for Falkner. A few times I had almost slipped and told her about my baby. I wanted her to know in the worst way but didn't think it fair for her to find out before Diarmuid.

As the wine was passed, I thought of all the couples blessed by the Goddess: Kyra and Falkner, Lyndon and Paige, Diarmuid and me. We had been together for over three months now, seeing each other nearly every day despite the obstacles. Last month we had celebrated the summer solstice by coming together in our circle, surrounded by red feathers for passion. I was more in love with him now than ever, still happy to guard our secret love, our secret child, but I had to admit, I wanted more. Watching a ceremony like tonight's, I realized that change must come. If we were to raise our child together, in a strong coven, it was time to reveal our love to our clans.

After the wine and cakes were passed around, the talk turned to spells to be cast and tales of witch hangings. One covener reported that a Wyndonkylle woman from a village to the south had been pulled from her home and charged with human sacrifice. She was still in prison—if the frightened guards had restrained themselves from burning her without trial.

"'Tis worse than you say," said Ian MacGreavy. "For that woman's coven believes that she was turned in to the authorities by two of our own! They're accusing Wodebaynes of naming her as a witch!"

"No!" everyone grumbled. "It can't be!"

"But there are no Wodebaynes residing in the south," said Falkner's mother.

"Aye, but at the time two of our own happened to be traveling south, right through the Wyndonkylles' village," the miller answered.

"Will we never have justice?" one elder railed. It was Howland Bigelow, an old woodcrafter. "Once again we're being blamed for someone else's evil! Why don't they just heap more condemnation upon our already burdened reputation?"

I felt the ire of the coveners rising as folks broke into smaller groups to tell their own tales of hateful acts against Wodebaynes. A few times in the past we had discussed bigotry in the circle, but never with this level of unrest and anger. The glitter of hatred in Ian MacGreavy's eyes harkened me back to the time I had witnessed him casting a dark spell, and I wondered if any of the other coveners had turned to black magick in private. Perhaps Aislinn, the young rebel, not much older than me, who often railed against the bigots who hated us?

I pressed a hand to my bodice, worried about the child within. I was convinced my bairn was a girl—another future high priestess. But she could not come into a world of hatred and chaos; this rancor had to subside before my child entered this life.

"'Twould be wise to calm your tempers and your fears," came a firm voice. Coveners looked to my mother, who spoke with the authority of the high priestess. "I daresay this is nothing new."

"But Síle, it's getting worse!" old man Bigelow claimed. "I've half a mind to cast a dark spell upon the Wyndonkylles to show them what real black magick is. We're taking the blame for it; we might as well do the deed!"

My mother remained quiet while people grumbled, then answered, "Howland, I know you are far too gentle a man to ever wish harm upon another."

"Oh, I can wish," he said. "I can wish the Goddess would send a mist over their fields to dampen the soil. Ruin their planting!"

"He's right!" Aislinn pushed into the center of the group. "Haven't we endured enough hatred? Isn't it time to fight back?"

People murmured in approval, nodding.

I couldn't believe how eager the folks in our coven were to engage in a war between clans. I winced, realizing how impossible it would be to see Diarmuid if we took to fighting.

"That is quite enough!" Síle said sternly.

The coveners fell silent as she demanded their attention. "We'll have no more talk of evil spells. Have you all forgotten your own initiation into the circle? Your vow to do the Goddess's will? Have you forgotten that you committed yourself to foster love and peace under the Goddess's sky?"

Aislinn tucked a loose tress of red hair behind her ear and

let out a disappointed sigh, but most of the others seemed thoughtful. They seemed to be listening to Ma's words.

"Remember the Witch's Rede?" Síle asked in a commanding voice. "Whatever you desire, whatever you ask of the Goddess, let it harm no one. And remember that as you give, so it shall return threefold."

"'Tis right thinking, Síle," Ian MacGreavy said. "This coven will never engage in dark magick, so 'tis futile to waste words upon it."

I looked at him in awe, remembering his own dark rite. What a hypocrite he was!

But Ma seemed satisfied as the coveners broke into small groups and talked of other matters. My mother had calmed the uproar, but discontent hung in the warm summer night. I worried that this could brew into a terrible storm and vowed to share my fears with Diarmuid.

The next morning as I went to meet Diarmuid, I felt a strange heaviness inside. The coven's anger was still roiling inside me, along with my breakfast. I realized that the sour feeling might be from carrying my baby. Perhaps there was a spell in Ma's Book of Shadows to alleviate it? I would have to take another look. I had been reading up on many of her spells lately—including one I wanted to try with Diarmuid. Although Ma had encouraged me to study her Book of Shadows, I didn't think she had expected me to find the entry on love magick. It claimed that couples sometimes made love in the center of the circle, offering their love force to the Goddess! Nothing like that had ever taken place in our coven circles, but I felt drawn to the idea of making love magick with Diarmuid.

I was also unsettled by the fact that I had lost my love charm. I had taken to carrying the rose stone in my pocket ever since Diarmuid and I first shed our clothes, but I had not come across it for weeks now. 'Twas not the best of days.

Diarmuid was in a far better mood. He chased me through the clearing, swiping at my skirts and wrestling me onto the grassy moss. The carefree play lifted my spirits, but after we kissed for a while, he sensed that something was wrong.

"Rose, there's no light in your eyes today. What is it, love?"

I told him about the trouble brewing between the Wyndonkylles and Wodebaynes.

"I've heard the same tale," he said. "But surely the Wodebaynes aren't involved."

"We are not, but we're being blamed, and I fear a storm brewing among the clans. A war that would destroy our chances of ever seeing each other again."

"I won't let that happen," he insisted.

"Then we must take action now." I paused, reluctant to push. "Let me ask you, Diarmuid, when you think of us, how do you picture us being together?"

"I have always wanted to marry you, Rose," he said, his eyes bright with promise. "Can't you see us two in the circle for a hand fasting?"

"I'll wager I've imagined it," I said, studying his beautiful face. "Oh, Diarmuid, we should marry. And soon. Let it happen now."

"Today?" he joked. "Let me run and fetch my ma, for she won't want to miss it."

"Would that it could happen so soon."

"Aye, sooner. That it happened yesterday and we're an old

married couple, with me poking around the cottage and asking you what's for dinner."

" 'Twould be a blessing. Far better than what I fear might happen."

"Stop that!" He pressed his hands over my eyes, then over my ears. "Don't listen to what the coven folk say. We are going to be married." He stood up and straightened his white shirt. "I'll go to my coven today and tell them everything. That I love you, that you're the best thing under the Goddess's blue sky, and that we're to be married."

"And if they argue that you're marrying a Wodebayne—"

"They won't. I will not give them the chance." He pulled me to my feet. "I love you, Rose. I'll make things right for us."

In that moment I knew he would. The Goddess had chosen a true hero for me.

I went up on my toes and kissed him. "And I have a spell to help us through. Have you ever heard of love magick?"

Diarmuid smiled. "No, but I think I will like it."

The spell in Ma's Book of Shadows was simple. I swept the circle and told Diarmuid to shed his clothes, lie back, and think of what we wanted to dedicate ourselves to.

When I had finished the preparations, I lay beside him, staring at the cloudy sky. "Picture us together," I whispered, "our union accepted by our clans, by all clans." I reached over and touched his shoulder. He quickly turned on his side and kissed me.

"Would we be together like this?" he asked.

"Aye, always."

"As close as this?"

"Aye," I whispered, focusing on our union, offering our act to the Goddess. Within the circle our bodies rose in heat and splendor, and I felt the glow of our love rising to the heavens.

"Aye, Goddess, we are here for You," I whispered as Diarmuid and I tumbled into passion.

Our love magick was strong. That night when I left our circle I heard thunder rumbling overhead. I felt sure the Goddess had received our offering. She was shaking up the heavens in preparation for Diarmuid's big announcement.

But the next day, when Diarmuid was to have met me at our secret place, he did not appear. Nor did he make it there the day after that. On the third day I sent him a tua labra: *Where are you? Why can you not meet your love?* But I received no response. I wondered whether he had received my message. Had something terrible happened? As each day passed, I waited for the rumble in the heavens to manifest itself on earth. Surely if I looked carefully, I would see Diarmuid tramping up the path to our cottage, his parents marching dutifully behind him, eager to work out with Síle the details of our union.

With the dawn of yet another morning I pushed open the shutter and peered out, longing for the glimpse of a Leapvaughn tartan or a flash of Diarmuid's lovely blue eyes. The path was still but for a jackrabbit searching for greens. My rescuer had not come for me . . . at least, I thought, not yet.

That afternoon Kyra and I went to the woods to gather fresh summer herbs. While Kyra was cutting clover, I went in search of clove, which was good for settling the stomach. When our pouches were full, we went to the circle Diarmuid and I had gathered in so many times. There, on the rock altar, we consecrated our herbs. As we finished, I noticed that Kyra had been unusually quiet today. I watched her sorting herb pouches in her basket, her chestnut hair braided into a twist at the top of her head.

"You know, with your hair up like that, you look like your ma," I said.

She smiled. "Falkner likes my hair free and loose, but 'tis too much to endure in this heat." Leaving her basket, she lifted my hair from my shoulders and waved it over my neck. "You'll roast under the sun with your hair down."

"I'll be fine."

"I must say I am worried about you, Rose. How many days has it been?"

I knew she was talking about how long since I'd seen Diarmuid. "Seven . . . no, eight."

"Eight days and you still believe he's coming back?"

"Of course he is. We rendered some powerful magick together, Kyra. Right here in this circle." My hair slipped out of her hands as I kicked off my shoes and walked the circle. I had come to know every tree root and dirt clod in this sacred place. I went over to the green moss that had often served as our bed and sat down. "The last time I saw him, we performed love magick. Did you hear the thunder in the sky that night? 'Twas us, devoting our love to the Goddess."

"I thought the rumbling was the sound of coming rain," Kyra said. "Rose, I really am worried about you."

"Don't despair for me," I said. "My Diarmuid will be here soon. You must help me plan the hand-fasting ceremony."

Kyra smiled. "I shall be so happy for you on your wedding day, Rose. That a Leapvaughn could love you so . . . 'tis truly the work of the Goddess."

I smiled back, trying not to worry. I didn't want to admit to Kyra that I had begun to wonder what had happened to

Diarmuid. Where was my love? Why was he taking so long to come to my clan and my coven and announce his intentions to marry me? I knew the Goddess intended us to be together, but my patience was beginning to wear thin.

We returned to my cottage and found it empty.

"Ma said she was going into Kirkloch today," I said, pouring two mugs of cool tea. We set my share of the herbs out to dry, then went outside to sit in the shady grass, hoping to catch a breeze. Kyra told me of her first kiss with Falkner and of how they now kissed constantly, as if they'd both had their first taste of honey cakes. As I listened, I stared intently at the edge of the cottage path, willing Diarmuid to appear.

And lo, as my eyes strained in the distance, I saw the brush move, giving way to a pair of feet.

"He's coming!" I cried, scrambling to stand and adjust my skirts. As I settled myself, I saw that it wasn't Diarmuid, but a young boy. "It's not him." My voice dropped off in disappointment.

"But it is a Leapvaughn," Kyra said excitedly. "Look at the plaid of his tartan."

"Indeed." My heart swelled as the young boy smiled at us shyly.

"I've a message here for Rose MacEwan."

"That's me," I said, coming forward to meet him.

He reached into his satchel and removed a piece of pressed linen, much like the parchment we used in our Books of Shadows. Handing it to me, he bowed. "Good day to you."

My heart swelled with joy as I held the note to my breast. "I can barely breathe!"

"Read it! Read it!" Kyra gasped.

I started to read. " 'My dearest Rose, it is with heavy heart that I write to you. I will always love you, but . . .' "

The words began to stick in my throat. I could not speak, but neither could I tear my eyes away.

> I have come to see that we can never be together. It was foolish of me to think we could marry, though I will ever think of you longingly in our special place of the forest. Think of me when you go there, for mine eyes will never feast on that place or on you again.
>
> Please, Rose, do not cry for me. There will be others for you. Perhaps a stout, hearty Wodebayne lad? In the meantime, the best thing you can do is forget me.
>
> Truly,
> Diarmuid

Pain cut me like a spear through the middle of my body. I folded myself over the note, collapsing onto the ground. Sobbing in the dirt, I was barely aware of Kyra fluttering about, trying to get me inside, to fetch some water, to stroke my hair.

Diarmuid was not coming.

He would not marry me.

My life was truly coming to an end.

The days were a blur of swallowed tears and pain. When Ma first found me abed in the cottage, she pressed her hand to my forehead in alarm. "Are you ill?" she asked, her eyes stricken with concern.

"Quite ill," I told her. "'Tis my digestion. Nothing tastes quite right anymore."

She quickly set about placing cool rags upon my head and wrists and making me a special potion to drink. I watched as she boiled together meadowsweet, mint, and catnip leaves and flowers. 'Twas a lesson in herbs, but a painful one. I didn't know how long I could pretend that all my pain was physical, but I couldn't begin to tell my mother the truth about Diarmuid.

My Diarmuid!

I was devastated. How could he turn away from me? I pressed my face to the pillow as a new round of tears racked my body. Ma kept asking me where it hurt, and I lied and said that the pain was in my belly. I couldn't bear to reveal that I was suffering a broken heart.

Kyra came to see me every day, bringing me flowers and fresh-baked biscuits that did sit well once swallowed. One afternoon Kyra stayed with me while Ma went out on an errand, and she encouraged me to throw on a summer shawl and venture outside the cottage for some fresh air.

The sun was hot, but there was a cooling breeze, making the heat tolerable. My body felt feeble, like a creaking old cart, but Kyra said that was from staying in bed so long. We sat under an ancient tree by the path.

"You cannot let one boy strike you down so," Kyra told me. "You'll forget about him in time."

"Never," I said, reaching to touch my belly. A tiny mound was growing there, though it was still too soon for anyone else to notice. "I cannot let Diarmuid go, for I am to have his child come Imbolc."

Kyra gasped. "A babe! 'Tis no wonder you're feeling ill."

"Aye, but Ma's teas of mint and meadowsweet have helped the illness in my body. 'Tis the pain in my heart that will not relent."

"Oh, Rose . . . poor Rose!" Kyra rubbed my back gently through the shawl. "To be with child! It must be terrible for you.

I wish you had told me earlier. I'll help you be rid of it. There are herbs that—"

"I want the child," I said.

She shook her head sadly. "Not here, not now? To bear a bastard child in these parts is dangerous. You'll be ostracized by everyone—even some in our own coven!"

Kyra was right. To give birth to a child out of wedlock was a sin shunned by all in the Highlands. My life would be ruined. I folded my arms across my belly. "'Twill be fine, for the child has a father. Diarmuid will come to me before Imbolc."

"And if he doesn't?"

I bit my lips tight, refusing to answer.

"No one has to know you lost the babe! I've heard you can brew a tea—"

"'Tis enough talk of that!" I insisted. "Diarmuid will be a father to my child." I drew the shawl around me closer. "I'm sure he would be here now if he knew. . . ." As my words trailed off, I realized I had stumbled upon the solution.

This baby would bring Diarmuid to me. Once he knew of its life, he would leap over the obstacles between us.

"That's it," I said, blinking. "I must tell him." I stood up, feeling strength rise within me. "I must go to him."

Kyra stared up at me, shaking her head.

"If I go to him with news of our child, surely he will think of a way for us to be together! He will be so overcome with joy, nothing will deter him."

"But the note . . ." Kyra stood up and brushed her skirts. "He said that . . ."

I waved her off. "He knew nothing of our child when he wrote that." I headed toward the cottage, thinking of the new possibilities. "Perhaps when his parents learn of our babe, they will soften, too. We could live with them. Or if they reject us, Diarmuid shall come live among the Wodebaynes. I know our coveners will be suspicious of him, but once they come to know him, they will accept him."

With each breath, the flush of health filled my body. I had been sick over Diarmuid, but the cure was within my grasp now. I could go to my love. And once he learned of the blessed child within my womb, he would welcome me with open arms.

The following day I set off in a horse-drawn cart toward Diarmuid's village of Lillipool. Falkner had managed to secure the cart and horse from his father's shop, and Kyra sat between us, warning of the punishment the three of us would face if our parents found out the true reason for our visit to Lillipool. She could be so mettlesome at times, though I did have her to thank for arranging for the cart. In my current condition, I was not sure I could walk all the way to Lillipool without incident.

Lillipool was considered to be a Christian village, though for some time our coven had known that the Vykrothes had a circle nearby and Leapvaughn sheepherders lived in cottages on its outskirts. There was the usual small church, which I assumed Diarmuid's clan attended to avoid persecution as witches. A mill cranked at the edge of the village. We passed by it, then came upon the village center. In Lillipool's small, dusty square, peddlers displayed their wares amidst clouds of blowing dirt. No one knew why grass refused to grow on the village green here, but my mother had once told me that although Leapvaughns have a gift for sales and carpentry, they were known to be barren farmers.

Falkner guided the wagon through the lane, stopping for passing villagers who paid us little mind. He brought the cart over to a small wagon at the end of the square, its side panel painted Ye Finest Wood Crafters. "I've got to pick up a table for Da," he said. "'Twill be a short while, if you want to walk around."

He helped us down from the cart, and we dusted our skirts and stepped forward gingerly, our arms linked.

"I hope he is here," I said. "His father likes him to tend the sheep, but Diarmuid prefers to spend his time in the village and at market."

Kyra nodded, averting her eyes as a tin peddler leered at her. "'Tis an odd village," she said. "Like a desert in the Highlands."

As we walked past a tinker's wagon, a cart laden with fruits, and another with an array of bonnets, I kept searching for Diarmuid. I spotted a lad who walked with the same gait and another who seemed to share his broad smile, but I did not see my love.

When we reached the end of the row of carts, I spied a head of gingery brown hair. It was feathered back from his face, revealing startling blue eyes and a smile that warmed my heart.

Diarmuid.

"There he is!" I gasped.

Kyra squeezed my arm. "You found him."

But he was not alone. A tall, swanlike girl with pale yellow hair walked beside him.

"Who is she?" Kyra muttered.

"I don't know. Perhaps a friend."

Kyra looked back toward the cart. "I'll go see if Falkner can find out."

I barely noticed that she had left my side. My Diarmuid was within reach, so close I could run into his arms, yet something kept me there, my feet mired to the ground. Who was the girl?

I watched in horror as she said something to him, making him laugh. It had all the markings of flirtation. But then he chucked her under the chin, seeming more like an older brother. An older woman came by and handed the girl a tart. She took a taste, then fed the rest to Diarmuid with her bare fingers.

Such an intimate gesture. And he took it from her hand, licking his lips. Oh, Goddess, what did it mean?

"Rose," Kyra said, softly resting her hand on my arm. " 'Tis terrible . . . your worst fears confirmed! She is Diarmuid's betrothed! They were promised to each other as children, and they are to be wed upon next Samhain!"

I shook my head. "An arranged marriage?" How could it be? Why had he never told me? I pressed my hands to my hot cheeks. If Diarmuid was promised to another, we had no chance of being married.

"Oh, Rose!" Kyra squeezed my arm. "Such dire news, and you with child . . ."

It couldn't be. My hands dropped to fists at my side, and for a moment I wanted to rush over and pummel him. Diarmuid was not the hero I had thought him to be. He had lied to me.

But then, he'd faced overwhelming obstacles. Perhaps he'd been trying to protect me from this until he sorted it out? And if his parents had arranged the marriage, that meant he'd had no choice. "So he doesn't love her," I said, thinking aloud. "And of course, his parents would want him to marry within his clan. I'm sure it's part of the reason they don't want him to marry me."

"Not really," Kyra said. "The girl's name is Siobhan MacMahon, and she is not a Leapvaughn, but a Vykrothe."

"An arranged marriage to someone from another clan?" Anger rose in my throat, hot and painful. His parents thought it acceptable for him to marry outside his clan but not to marry me? Or was it that he could not marry a Wodebayne?

"Falkner has the table loaded in the cart," Kyra said. "He's ready to leave."

"But I haven't . . ." I glanced over at Diarmuid. Siobhan still hovered about him like a bee collecting nectar from a flower. It was hardly the time to march over and tell the boy I was going to bear his child.

This meeting had not worked out the way I'd planned. Not at all.

"Rose, you're crying," Kyra said gently.

"No matter." I swiped the tears out of my eyes with the backs of my hands. I needed to see him with her. I needed to see the enemy.

I stared at the swan-necked girl who was fawning over Diarmuid. She was tall and lithe, with flaxen gold hair. Everything about her was the physical opposite of me.

Diarmuid could not love one so unlike me. How could it be, Goddess? How was it possible that he could love another at all?

"We'd better go," Kyra said.

I felt her clamp my arm and pull me away toward the cart, my eyes still on Diarmuid's betrothed. How could he even think of marrying another?

How could he?

9.
On the Making and Charming of Poppets

I promised myself I would cry no more. Everyone knew too much sobbing could harm the child in a mother's womb, and I was beginning to learn that tears were futile. I needed to do something to secure my baby's happiness and health.

It was time to use my powers.

Why had I not thought of this before? I wondered as I steadfastly sewed and decorated my poppets, working a little each day and night. The course of my relationship with Diarmuid ran parallel to my magick. Had I not captivated him completely with the rose stone? And then, when I'd misplaced it, he had fallen away, never returning to our secret circle. It was so clear. I needed to enlist the Goddess's help to get him back in my arms.

I went through Ma's cupboard of stones, searching for a gem to replace the rose stone. I weighed each stone in my palm and turned it about, hoping to feel a swell or glow of power, but nothing moved me. Perhaps a charm wasn't the right thing anymore. Time for a spell.

First I dedicated a candle to him, carving runes up the side that spelled his name. Although I had to hide the candle from Ma, I burned it whenever she went out, chanting to the Goddess to rekindle the love flame in this boy. And when the flame was doused, I censed my belly with the smoke, inviting my babe to feel my love for her father.

While working candle magick, I also searched for a powerful love spell. Although Ma had instructed Kyra on the making of love dolls, I could not recall the details. Searching my mother's Book of Shadows, I came across the spell. It was called simply Poppets.

> *Thou must craft two poppets to represent the two lovers. What is done to the poppets shall be done to the lovers.*
>
> *Cut two pieces of cloth shaped like a man, then two shaped like a woman. While cutting the cloth, bring to mind the person it represents. If the ideal lover has long, flowing hair or a comely beard, so should the poppet. Thou must heed—the lover thou seekest is thine ideal mate, not a named lord or lady.*
>
> *Stuff the figure with herbs governed by Venus. Such herbs: verbena, feverfew, yarrow, motherwort, rosebuds, or damiana.*
>
> *'Tis strong magick! Use only for a love that will have permanence, not for a mere dalliance.*
>
> *Thou must thrice perform a love ritual over the poppets during the waxing moon.*

The spell was very specific and promised to be very powerful. And I would give it all the more power by making my doll look just like Diarmuid and embroidering his name upon it. My own brand of magick had worked well when charming the rose stone; I felt sure this would be even stronger.

It took me days to construct the dolls, during which Ma noticed and encouraged my work. "You are seventeen years of age, Rose. Perhaps 'tis time for you to fall in love with a gentle witch." She didn't see the name I had stiched upon it, didn't realize that I was making a Diarmuid poppet, designed to capture *his* love, and I didn't dare tell her that I was working magick she considered to be dark. When the dolls were done, I had to wait for the waxing moon to begin the spell. I felt impatient, but I knew that the spell would have its full potency only if I followed the instructions.

By the time I was ready to perform the spell for the third time, it was August and Lughnassadh preparations were upon us. During the weeks of preparing the dolls and consecrating them, I missed Diarmuid desperately. My only consolation was that we would have the rest of our lives together once we made it past this obstacle. I also noticed that the babe was growing, pushing at the swath of cloth I belted around my skirts. I had to adjust the girdle higher, which only seemed to accent the new lushness of my breasts. Perhaps this was the Goddess's purpose in waiting—to give Diarmuid a visible sign of my love for him, the child within my womb.

10.

Lughnassadh

Rising before dawn on the day of Lughnassadh, the celebration to honor the Sun God, I set off to my secret circle to complete the love spell. As I had done before, I placed the poppets facedown on the stone altar and consecrated the circle. I charged the girl poppet to be me, then picked up the boy, with feathery brown hair made of spun wool. Sprinkling it with salted water and censing it, I chanted: "This poppet is Diarmuid, my mùirn beatha dàn in every way. As Diarmuid lives, so lives this poppet. Aught that I do to it, I do to him."

I kissed the Diarmuid poppet, then put him back beside the other on the altar. Kneeling before them, I moved the two poppets closer to each other, touching, turning, pressing face-to-face. As I moved them, I pictured myself reaching out to Diarmuid, meeting him, touching him, kissing and holding him so close in my arms, I could taste the salt on his skin.

When the poppets were face-to-face, I wrapped my red ribbon around them. "Now may the Goddess bind these two together, as I do bind them here," I said. Around and around I circled them with ribbon, then tied it tightly so they would never, ever break apart. "Now they are forever one. May each truly become a part of the other. Separated, they shall seem incomplete. So mote it be!"

I rested my athame over the bound puppets, asking the Goddess to lend Her power to this and all spells I cast. Then I wrapped the poppets in a clean white cloth. I would stow them in the rafters of the cottage so that no animal or human could meddle with my magick.

After my task was done, I lifted my head to the bright mid-day sky. The heat was blistering hot today, casting a white glow across the land. Aye, 'twas the right day to honor the Sun God. I would go to Lillipool, but not until the sun had passed. 'Twas best not to make such a journey in the heat. Besides, of late my babe had drained me of strength. I no longer needed special herbs to calm my dizziness, but it seemed the babe wanted me to sleep the day away! I needed rest and a sip of cool tea.

By late afternoon, when the air had cooled and Ma was off preparing for the Lughnassadh celebration, I knew 'twas time to go. As I walked, I chanted bits and pieces of the love spell. "Now may the Goddess bind these two together, as I do bind them here. . . . Separated they would seem incomplete. . . ." The spell sustained me, and in no time the old mill of Lillipool loomed before me.

Today I was not so lucky as to find him in the dusty mar-ketplace. I knew his coven would also be preparing to cele-brate the sun festival, but what were his assigned tasks? To mull the wine—or consecrate the circle? I wouldn't dare go near another coven's circle, not that I would be able to find it.

Help me, Goddess, I prayed. Point me in the direction of my love.

I circled the dismal marketplace, hoping for an answer. Diarmuid did not appear, but as I paced, I came across a red feather. It sat in the middle of the lane, alone and abandoned, and the sight of it reminded me of the red feathers twined with ivy that I had used for our celebration of midsummer night. I had twined ivy around the feathers—red for sexuality—and festooned them around our circle.

Now this feather pointed down a lane. Was it pointing me toward my love?

I believed it to be so. Making haste, I followed the lane, which led past the church and quaint cottages to the countryside. My eyes followed the dark green patches of grass to a small hollow where a figure lay sleeping in the shade.

Diarmuid.

He was probably supposed to be tending sheep, though this summer heat would drive any lad to napping. I ventured off the road and crossed to him, my shoes whispering in the crisp grass. Although I did not call out to him, he stirred with my approach, rubbing his eyes. He turned toward me, saw me, then bolted upright.

"What vision is this?" he gasped. "Has the Goddess herself descended, or am I but asleep and dreaming of love?"

My heart melted. He was still the same Diarmuid, a poet and a tease.

"I have come to reclaim you," I said firmly.

He took my hand and lifted it to his lips. "You will always have my heart, Rose."

"I want more," I said, thrilled by the spark of his lips upon my hand. "We summoned the Goddess to bless our union, and she did. She looks down upon us with favor, yet you allow another to become your betrothed?"

He stared at the ground. "'Twas not my doing, Rose."

"Do you not remember your last words to me? That we were to be married forthwith?"

"I do," he said sheepishly. "But 'tis not so simple a matter."

"Aye, there are complications, but I have come to help you through them."

His blue eyes sparkled with regret. "I'm afraid you can't help, Rose. No one can help me. I have learned that a man cannot cross his elders or defy his clan. I need the approval of my coven, and they have vowed not to give it."

"Aye, I face the same challenges," I said, thinking of my ma and the coveners who wanted to rail against rival clans. "But this is no surprise, Diarmuid. We talked of it often. 'Twill not be easy, but you must remain steadfast and strong, lower your head and charge, like the ram in yonder field."

"Would that I were a ram, destined to chew grass and laze in the sun." He reached for his throat and nervously squeezed the pentagram concealed by his shirt. "Instead I am a marriageable lad, a property of my parents dangled like a carrot before a horse."

"Tell me you don't love her," I said.

"She has her fair attractions," he said, cutting me.

My knees nearly buckled beneath me. Was this my love, the one who had pledged his love in the Goddess's circle? He had promised to love me and only me. He was supposed to see only my charms.

Did he kiss her the way he had kissed me? Did he touch her and . . . oh, excruciating torture! I could not think of such things now. Think of the spell, I told myself. Your reason for being here—your baby.

"But mostly, it is the ease with which my life will progress if I take her hand."

His words gave me some relief. I realized it was time to tell him. "Yet I offer not a life of ease, but a sign of our bond." Boldly I took his hand and placed it on my belly. "There is a child within, Diarmuid. Do you feel it stirring?"

He gasped, stepping closer to me. There was power in his touch, magnified all the more by the glow of the child growing inside me.

"The Goddess has given us a babe, a sign of our union. 'Twill be the child that unites the Wodebaynes and the Leapvaughns. Perhaps our child will unite all clans. Oh, Diarmuid, this is how the Goddess intended it. Could you deny such a powerful destiny?"

"I could not," he gasped. "I will not." His face softened as he stroked my belly. "A man does not abandon his child, no matter what the obstacles."

My spirits lifted. He understood. He knew that our baby was a sign from the Goddess.

"We must marry now—today!" he said, pulling me into his arms for a kiss. Then he pulled away and dropped to his knees to kiss my belly. "My child. Goddess be praised!" He kissed the baby over and over again.

I smiled. "How would you marry? In a church? Or do you think one of our covens would add a highly unusual hand fasting to the Lughnassadh rites?"

"We'll do it any way we can," he insisted. "Mayhap your village is best, away from Siobhan and my family. We'll go to the Presbyterian reverend first—tonight. Surely he will help us."

My heart lifted. Diarmuid was coming home with me. We would be together—married!

"After that we'll arrange a hand fasting," he went on. "No one dare deny us once we're together. I must first run home for a few belongings, then I shall meet you." He glanced up, gauging the position of the sun. "Let us meet at our circle in the woods before the sun sets."

I put my hand in his hair, loving the feel of it. "Would that we could travel together."

"Aye, but your presence would raise too much of a stir at my cottage right now. We'll meet in the woods at our circle before sunset." He stood up and kissed me again. "Oh, Rose, you are the world to me. After today we shall never be separated again."

"Never," I said, thinking of the words of the love spell. "Never."

The journey back to my own woods was cooled by afternoon breezes and dreams of lingering in Diarmuid's arms. On the way I stopped at the brook for a drink of water, then headed off to prepare the circle for our formal reunion. I swept the circle, then decided to rest on the moss for a while, as the long journeys had taken their toll on my strength. I sat there chanting from the love spell and picturing Diarmuid in my bed each morning when I arose. Where would we live? Perhaps Ma would have us once she got over her initial anger. Besides, she would want to be near the babe, to help nurse her, then to teach her the ways of the Goddess as she grew older. Listening to the sounds of the woods—to the trill of birds and the rustle of wind in the trees—I dozed off.

When I awoke, it was dark but for the sickly glow of a yellow moon.

Where was Diarmuid? I sat up suddenly, and my sacred place seemed like a strange wilderness. My life force hammered in my chest as reality hit me.

He was not here. Was he coming?

What had happened? "Oh, Goddess, keep and protect him," I whispered, sure that something dreadful had happened to him. There could be no other explanation. I had seen the determination in his eyes, I had felt his commitment. Nothing could stay him from me. Nothing but . . . something terrible and evil.

I stood up, brushing dust and seeds from my hair. I would return to Diarmuid's village. I had surely missed the coven circle, but I planned to miss many more in my life with Diarmuid. Who knew where our adventures would take us? And right now he needed me. I had to go to him.

Darkness closed in around me as I crept through the woods, following my familiar landmarks to the road. I started on my way, wending over a rise. Glancing up, I saw a girl my own age approaching.

Swanlike neck. Flaxen hair.

Siobhan MacMahon.

I was gripped by hatred for her—everything about her, from her sun-kissed hair to her long, graceful neck. But as she caught sight of me, I realized that perhaps I was being unfair. Perhaps, in Diarmuid's troubles, he had sent her to come for me. Perhaps she was the messenger of my love. I stepped toward her, eager for news.

"Hark!" I called out to her. "Have you come in search of me, Rose MacEwan?"

"Aye." She drew close, a sourness pinching her mouth. "I have come in search of Diarmuid's harlot."

I felt stung.

"I have just come from him, the poor lad," she said. "He was about to ruin his life by running off with a woman who could satisfy only his base desires. A Wodebayne! Such foolishness. I stopped him in the nick of time."

"How did you stop him?" I asked, afraid of the harm she might have done to him. "Did you hurt him?"

" 'Twas not necessary. I needed only to sate his desires to remind him of his attraction to me. He's fine. Sleeping like a babe, if you must know."

I felt my hands clenching into fists at the implications. Had she lain with him? I could not believe it to be true. He had sworn to be my first and last love and I his. "I don't believe you," I said. "I do not believe a word you are saying."

"Aye, but then, you Wodebaynes aren't bright, are you? That's what I told him. Why throw away a beautiful life with me so that you can waste away with a savage, uneducated Wodebayne?"

"Perhaps he does not want to be counted among warmongers like the Vykrothes?" I jabbed.

She cocked her head, as if weary. "He is perfectly fine with my clan. That's part of his problem. Diarmuid gets on with everyone. At least, every lass. I guess you might call it the charm of the Leapvaughns. They do like to trick us. You are not his first little mistake, you know. He has had others before you." She folded her arms contentedly. "But he always comes back to me."

A mistake? A trick? Her words darted through the air like arrows. I sized her up. If I were to battle her, I felt, I would win, and the temptation to cast her to the ground was irresistible.

"How dare you!" I seethed, reaching for her arm.

Siobhan stepped away, avoiding me. "Take heed." She smiled

like a cat who has fallen but landed on her feet. "You cannot fight the forces at work here. He and I were promised by our parents long ago. 'Twas a plan to unite the Vykrothes and Leapvaughns. And although my Diarmuid has strayed with the likes of you, he always comes back to me." Her pale gray eyes were full of spite. "He loves me. You are just a passing fancy."

"So you say," I said tartly, though I felt my strength washing away in the rising tide of doubt. I stood there, trying to fight the feelings that swept through me at the implication that Diarmuid had lain with another, perhaps many others. *Oh, Goddess!* I wanted to fall to the ground and sob but wouldn't give Siobhan the satisfaction of witnessing my fully blossomed pain.

Would he betray me?

Would he lie with another?

Oh, Diarmuid . . .

"I've come here not to fight with you, but to give you a warning," Siobhan went on. "I know of your silly magick and your Wodebayne tendency to turn to the dark forces." She reached into her pocket and took out a small object. She held it up to the moon, then tossed it to my feet.

The rose stone! How had she come to have it?

"It is worthless now," she said. "I saw to that."

The small stone looked dim and gray in the dust of the road. I felt too startled to pick it up or respond.

"Stay away from Diarmuid, or you will regret it for as long as you live." With that, Siobhan turned away and marched off toward Lillipool.

I stared after her in utter shock. Ordering me away from my love? Crossing my magick charm! Defying the Goddess! Malice rose within me, churning, burning. The urge to shoot dealan-dé at her made my hands twitch. I lifted my hand . . .

But she turned back with a scowl.

I held the fire within me, held on to the desire to blast her in the face. "You haven't seen the end of me!" I shouted. "You will not have Diarmuid, and you will pay for foiling our plans."

Siobhan laughed. It was a cruel, cold sound that seemed to dance on the summer breeze. She was still laughing when she turned away and strode off. Even from behind, her long neck and pale beauty were regal and comely. I wished she would shape-shift into a fat swan and fly away!

There in the center of the road, I stretched my arms out to the Goddess and lifted my face to the sky. I was so frustrated! Why did I keep losing my love at every turn? Despite Diarmuid's weaknesses, I knew the Goddess intended us to be together. I knew he was destined to be a father to the child in my womb.

The moon above me was ringed with a watery halo—a sign of disruption. As I watched, it moved like a ring of oil, snaking in and out. A ring of madness. It made me wary. Nothing in the air tonight was reliable. It was a moon of illusions and interruptions. I half expected the ground beneath my feet to buckle and give way, dropping me deep into an earthly grave.

Oh, what was I doing, suffering hysterics here in the middle of the road, where murderers, thieves, and disapproving Christians could come along at any second? Overwhelmed, I moved off the road to hide behind some bushes, pressed my palms to my face, and began to cry. It was too much to bear— losing my love again! And it hurt all the more now that he knew of our child. He was not just turning against me: he was rejecting the tiny babe in my womb!

I was on my knees, sobbing, when I sensed another blood

witch in the brush behind me. I turned and stared into the darkness, using my magesight. Aislinn, the young witch from Síle's coven, was closing in on a rabbit. She leapt into a patch of watery moonlight, trying to catch it, but the animal slipped away at the last second.

She was probably on her way home from the Lughnassadh circle, but what was she doing trying to catch a rabbit? "Aislinn?" I called through my tears. "What are you doing?" Could she be trying to capture a creature to spill its blood in a dark spell?

"Oh, just having a game with the creature," Aislinn said, closing the distance between us. Her mouth twitched a bit, making me wonder if my suspicions were correct. "What say you, Rose? Your ma said you were ill, but here, collapsed along the road?" She hurried over and helped me to my feet. "Can you walk?"

"I think so," I said, "though I have nowhere to go now that . . ." A new wave of hysteria came over me, and I choked on my words.

Aislinn patted my back. "Come now, Rose. I've never seen you in such a state. We must sit." She led me to a fallen log, where we sat amid the fireflies. "We missed you at the circle tonight, and I know your ma was worried, though she made your excuses, claiming that your sickness had arisen once again. I sense that it is not sickness that kept you away, but some other distressing matter."

As she talked, I dried my eyes with the hem of my summer skirt. When she pushed back her red hair, I noticed that she had inscribed runes of plant dye on her forehead as part of her devotion to the Sun God. I gasped. It was typical Aislinn, but Reverend Winthrop of the village would have her hanged for the pagan practice if he saw the markings. It seemed as though she were risking her life to flaunt her devotion to the Goddess. Aislinn had always been a rebel, and I found much of her behavior shocking. I was not sure that I could trust her, but she was a member of my coven, and at the moment I had so few choices.

"You have guessed right," I told her. "It seems I am caught in a terrible love triangle, and I have spent the evening grappling with a vicious Vykrothe girl who intends to steal my love away!"

Her face was awash with moonlight and interest, so I told her of my sorrows. Of my love for Diarmuid despite our clan differences. Of his intentions to run away with me. Of Siobhan's interference. I managed to exclude mention of my baby, not wanting to give Aislinn more than her share of sordid details. And it seemed that her ardor was fired by the situation alone.

"Yet another example of the other clans conspiring against us!" she railed. "Oh, you poor girl! To be the victim of their hatred."

I felt new tears slip down my cheeks at her words. At the moment I didn't care so much about the hatred among the clans, I just wanted Diarmuid back.

"I don't blame you for crying," Aislinn said. Her red hair fell over one cheek like a thick veil as she leaned toward me. "It's a heavy burden upon your shoulders now, made all the worse by the fact that your ma doesn't understand at all. She keeps telling Wodebayne folks to lie down while the other clans trample over us!"

I sniffed, surprised that Aislinn understood how difficult it was to be the daughter of a high priestess, especially one with such strong views. Although the Wodebaynes had endured bigotry throughout my life, my mother had never wavered from her position of peace among the clans. I wondered about Ma now. She would be annoyed at my disappearance.

But her true fury would pour out when she learned of my love for a boy from another clan and of my pregnancy.

Pressing a hand against my belly, I realized I would have to return to Síle tonight. It was late, and it would be far too dangerous, not to mention foolhardy, for me and my babe to try and make the journey into Lillipool tonight.

Oh, how had I gotten myself into such a position?

"You cannot let this matter rest," Aislinn said, her eyes lit with determination.

"Aye, my heart will not let me." Nor will the child inside me, I thought as I slid off the log.

"You must fight back," Aislinn went on. "Síle and her coveners keep trying to tamp down the fires, but there's no quenching the blaze now. The other clans have struck the first blows, and now it's up to us to show them the strength of our magick. We have the power to punish the other clans. Why don't we use it?"

"Indeed." For once I agreed with Aislinn. I had borne so many slights as a result of hatred against the Wodebaynes. It was all too much. I could barely hold my head steady as I started to trundle home.

"I will see you home," Aislinn said, slipping an arm around my waist. "We'll talk more when you're feeling better."

Grateful for the firm hand at my waist, I tried to concentrate on making my way home. What would I say to Ma when I got there, and how would she react?

I meandered up the path to Ma's cottage cautiously, expecting her to fly out the door and have at me. But the cottage was silent and dark, and when I opened the door, I saw that Ma was not there. I stepped inside the shadowed house and slipped off my shoes, greatly relieved. Sleep could not come soon enough. Wanting nothing more than to fall into bed, I removed the girdle at my waist and slipped off my light summer gown. Standing before the washbasin, I tipped the water pitcher over it to rinse my face and hands . . .

And out hopped a frog.

I shrank back. A frog? In the cottage? As I went to light a candle from the fire, I heard a croak. And when I turned back toward the room, I saw them—frogs everywhere! Bumpy, spotted frogs dotted the floor, rode the chairs, perched on the bed.

I shrieked. They were surrounding me! How had they gotten in here?

Feeling as if I had nowhere to turn, I grabbed the broom, threw open the door, and began to coax them out. "Begone!" I said. "Back to where you belong!" I didn't want to harm the Goddess's creatures, but their presence unnerved me. I scooted them off the bed, pushed them from the chairs, swept them across the floor. The fat, slimy creatures burped in response. I swung the broom, sending them hopping. "Begone!" I cried through tears of frustration.

As I shooed out a tiny creature who seemed determined to turn back, I noticed a lantern bobbing along the path. It was Ma. Her face seemed placid, even amused as she ventured closer for a better look. She eyed the creatures now dotting the path to our cottage. "Frogs?"

"The cottage was riddled with them when I returned."

"What sort of infantile spell is this?" she asked, stepping aside as a frog skittered out the door.

A spell! Of course. 'Twas a spell from Siobhan, the wicked wench.

"I haven't seen the likes of it since I was a young girl," Ma said. " 'Tis a silly little thing, usually in a child's Book of Shadows."

I stopped sweeping as a tear rolled down to my chin and fell, plopping onto a frog. Suddenly something inside me snapped, and my tears turned to laughter. The tear-struck creature hopped out the door, croaking its complaint.

Ma laughed, too, and we fell together, embracing in the midst of the ludicrous scene. Soon after, we recovered enough to shoo the remaining frogs out the door. As Ma moved about with the lantern, checking the corners of the cottage for stragglers, she spoke. "I have been worried about you. I was just out searching, knowing how unlike you it is to miss a Greater Sabbat. Are you ill?"

" 'Tis terrible, Ma," I said. "Though I am not ill." I sat down at the table and told her. I told her how I had fallen in love with someone from another clan, another coven, and how I had lost my Leapvaughn love because of his arranged marriage to a Vykrothe. I told her everything—omitting only the mention of the babe, for 'twould be too much to lay upon her in one sitting.

" 'Tis no wonder I've been concerned," Ma said. "I knew you were carrying a heavy load these days, though I did not know the specifics." She stood up from the table and went over to her cupboard of magickal things. "I must admit, Rose, I was quite alarmed to discover this just before I left for the Sabbat." From the cupboard she removed a white satchel. No, not a satchel—a white cloth. She lifted it to reveal the two poppets I'd made! But they were no longer bound together with red ribbon! They were separated. Ma placed them on the table between us.

"Where did you find these?" I asked.

"On the floor."

They must have dropped out of the rafters! And Ma had been the one to cut them apart. "Why did you meddle with them?" I asked. "Why did you foil the magick?"

"I was going to leave them together until I noticed the runes you'd embroidered upon them." She held up the one that said Diarmuid. "You put a boy's name on this! Truly, Rose, you know it's wrong. I've said that time and again. This is dark magick, and I'll not have it coming from my daughter, or any Wodebayne, if I can prevent it."

The sight of the unbound poppets frustrated me so, I barely heard her words. So my spell had worked until Ma had discovered the dolls and separated them. I felt fresh anger, this time at Síle. She was putting her beliefs about magick before me.

And what of Diarmuid's own love for me? Was it not strong enough to see our marriage through without help of my magick? It was all so confusing.

"Rose . . ." Ma's voice interrupted my thoughts. "You're not listening! You have no right to tamper with that boy's destiny! It may seem like 'tis the easy way out, but your intrusive spell will come back to haunt you—threefold! And I worry about you tangling with a Vykrothe girl. They are a fierce tribe, and you have a history with them that I've dared not speak of before this."

"I do?" I winced. "When did I engage a Vykrothe?"

"Do you remember your trip to the coast with your father?" she asked. When I nodded, she went on. "While you were there, the rains fell, causing terrible coastal flooding. Many of the neighboring Vykrothe homes and fields were flooded . . . ruined. And there's rumor that the floods came as a result of a spell cast by your father."

"So Da did practice dark magick?"

Ma sighed deeply. "I do not think so, but that is how the rumor goes. They say there was an angry confrontation between Gowan and a Vykrothe man in a village inn. As a result, they say, your father cast a black spell upon the village. . . . Hence the flooding."

"Did you ever ask Da about it?"

Ma looked down. "I didn't even know of the flooding at the coast until after your da was gone."

I shook my head. "'Tis quite a tale."

"Aye, that's what I believe it to be—a fanciful tale." Ma rose from the table and poured fresh water into the basin. "Now, off to bed. We'll talk more of this come the morning."

I washed off and curled onto my sleeping pallet. Sleep would come quickly, I knew, as my body and mind were worn weary. But as I drifted off, the image of Aislinn popped into my head. Her fiery red hair was aglow in the moonlight, her eyes wild. "We have the power to punish the other clans," she'd said. "Why don't we use it?"

Because power could be dangerous? But witches wielded the Goddess's power all the time. Did not the Goddess impose her own sense of justice? Besides, I had not cast the spell of frogs. And I had not stolen another's love away. Diarmuid had pledged himself to me under the Goddess; his bond with Siobhan was a business matter determined by his parents. Could I not defend myself against this vengeful girl? I was merely protecting myself and my babe. Even as my father might have defended himself from a Vykrothe all those years ago.

It was all too much to sort out this night. I yawned as Ma

came close, tucking a light blanket over me. "Good night, Rose. We'll undo your spell in the morn."

Mayhap, I thought. Or mayhap I would find a way to cast a new spell upon Diarmuid. I breathed softly, feeling coddled by her love. 'Twas a lovely feeling for now, but I knew it would not sustain me.

I had reached a time when a mother's love was not enough.

I needed Diarmuid.

The next day the Sun God sent splinters of sunlight into the cottage. The light awakened me, infusing my body with refreshed strength and hope. I thought of the words from the Lughnassadh rites.

> *"Goddess, we thank thee*
> *for all that has been raised from the soil.*
> *May it grow in strength*
> *from now till harvest.*
> *We thank thee for this promise of fruits to come."*

I rubbed my belly. My baby had been but a seed at Beltane, but 'twould be a fine child to be born around the time of the Imbolc rites.

Grow in peace, little one, I thought as I rose from my bed. Your ma will take care of these difficult matters and bring your da to you.

That morning I enlisted Kyra's help in fighting the battle. I knew if I wanted to get to Diarmuid, I would first have to stave off Siobhan.

"A minor spell is necessary," I told Kyra. "Something to

scare her off." After some thought I added, "Something to mar her lovely golden hair." We were sitting in my sacred circle, trying to remember anything we'd ever heard of dark spells. This was not the sort of thing you learned at the circle or looked up in your mother's Book of Shadows.

"I've heard tell of turning a person's nails black," she said. "Or perhaps you can send a lightning bolt upon her head?"

"That's a bit too much," I said. "I can't be causing her serious harm, though I must say, 'tis tempting." We meandered through the woods, talking about what we knew of herbs and spells. When we came upon a thorny plant, I went over and circled it with my bolline. "'Tis just the thing to tangle her lovely hair. Can you imagine Siobhan stuck among a bramble of thorns?" On the way back to my altar I cut a lovely purple iris to give me the wisdom to work a new spell. Working together, Kyra and I swept the circle and consecrated the thorns. Then I made up a chant:

> *"O Goddess of Light, Goddess so fair,*
> *Please bring these thorns upon her hair.*
> *Let Siobhan know my wrath,*
> *Let her nevermore cross my path!"*

"So mote it be!" Kyra said, her eyes lit with expectation.

Afterward we could barely contain our curiosity. Would our spell be a success?

"Perhaps we should go and see with our own eyes," I said. "Besides, I am due a trip to Lillipool. I must speak to Diarmuid and try to work things out."

Kyra tucked a cornflower behind her ear. "Perhaps we

should pay a visit to Falkner at his father's shop? If he can get use of a horse, we'll be in Lillipool in no time."

I smiled. "Is it because you want to see the spell or because you want to see Falkner?"

A mischievous gleam danced in her eyes. "Both!"

At the Kirkloch blacksmith's shop we found Falkner, who talked his da into making a run to a merchant in Lillipool. Falkner had met Siobhan at market on more than one occasion. "That one thinks she's the queen of the Highlands," he said, rolling his eyes. "'Twould be quite satisfying to see her get her comeuppance."

In no time we were in the dusty Leapvaughn village, searching the marketplace for Diarmuid. It turned out that he was off tending sheep in the hills, but Falkner managed to learn the location of Siobhan's cottage. We left the horse tethered near a water trough in the village and went out to the MacMahon cottage on foot. The house was a small affair, overlooking a field of dry heather that gave way to a bog. The shutters had been thrown open from the windows, and smoke rose from the chimney.

We perched on a nearby hillside, just behind a fallen log.

"Is she home?" Kyra asked. "I don't see anyone about."

"I don't know," Falkner said, "but I cannot stay here watching a lone cottage all afternoon. Da's got work to be done. Besides, 'tis deadly dull."

"A bit of waiting would be well worth the sight of seeing Siobhan in distress," I said, watching the cottage.

Over in the bogs a few birds squawked. It was a lazy, still August afternoon. "Perhaps we could take turns napping while we wait?" I added.

Just then the wind kicked up over the heather, rattling through the weeds. It swept up from the bogs, bypassing our little hill but heading straight toward the cottage. As it churned, it blew seeds and thistle toward the house.

The door of the cottage swung open, and Siobhan flew out in a fury.

"There she is!" Kyra cried.

With her skirts gathered high Siobhan raced about the cottage, trying to shutter the windows. She pressed a shutter closed, but the strong wind sucked it back open. She reached for the shutter again, but dust and thistles and seed clods were swarming to her face, forcing her to cower. The thorny seeds blew directly upon her, hooking onto her skirts and apron. Dozens of burrs snagged in her hair, but when she reached up to tug them out, they pierced her fingertips.

"Eeow! Ow! Ooh!" she yelped, dancing about as the thorny seeds flew under the straps of her sandals.

"Ha!" I laughed with satisfaction. The three of us no longer hid behind the log but sat up for the best view of our quarry.

"Oh, Goddess, look at her!" Kyra laughed with me. "She's a sorry sight."

"From what I know of her, she quite deserves it," Falkner said. "I never thought I'd see the likes of her yelping about."

"Indeed," I said as Siobhan continued to hop around, pulling burrs from her clothes and hair. "At least this should stop her from sending more spells my way." And, I thought, perhaps it will keep her away from Diarmuid, too!

"Oh, dear," Kyra said, her hand flying to her mouth. "She sees us! She's coming this way."

I arose and stood tall, not afraid of this petty Vykrothe whore.

"It's you!" Siobhan yelped, stomping toward me. "This is your magick, is it not?"

"Aye, though I must admit, I had to practice restraint," I said. "It's far less than you deserve."

"Blast you all!" Siobhan said, raising a fist in the air. "I'll curse you and your families, too!" She was quite a sight, her blond hair matted and tangled like so many rough cuttings of dirty wool. She moved without grace, as if every turn pained her.

'Twas satisfying indeed.

"Easy!" Falkner stepped toward her and gently touched her shoulder. "Easy, now! You rail like a savage beast. Perhaps you're in need of soothing!"

"Don't touch me!" she shrieked, stepping away from him. "I'll have you know that I'm betrothed, and you must mind your hands."

Falkner lifted his hands defensively. "I apologize! I was just trying to help."

"Take your leave, all of you!" Siobhan cried as she turned back to the cottage. "Begone, you and your vicious spells."

"Likewise to any witch who would summon frogs from the pond," I called to her.

As Siobhan slammed into the cottage, I turned to my friends. "That was worth waiting for, and you'll be back to your da's shop in no time," I told Falkner.

"But wait!" he said mysteriously. He held out one hand as if he were cradling an invisible tool.

"What's this?" Kyra said. "More magick?"

He smiled. "When I touched Siobhan's shoulder, I managed to extract a valuable item—a strand of her hair." He waved his closed fingers before me, and I saw it—a thin line of gold.

I was most impressed. All this time I had thought Falkner a bit dim-witted, but perhaps he had simply been keeping his thoughts to himself. In any case, I had to admire his foresight in stealing something that could prove quite valuable—especially if I needed to cast another spell against Siobhan. "Thank you," I said, sweeping the golden hair from his hand and tucking it into a tiny pouch from my pocket.

Kyra brushed off her skirts as we headed back toward the center of Lillipool. "That was amusing indeed, though I think Siobhan is a waste of your time and power," she told me. "You need to go directly to Diarmuid. Speak to him. The true power is with him, not that silly girl."

"I do believe you are right," I said as we walked along. "And I shall go to him tonight when he has returned from the fields. The Goddess will give him the strength to defy his name and clan. I know it to be our destiny."

I could not wait for the evening.

11.
Spelling a Death Drink with Dark Powers

Falkner delivered me to the path to Ma's cottage, and I waved good-bye to my friends with a firm resolution to work things out before nightfall. But as I neared the clearing, I noticed a group of coveners lingering outside our cottage. Panic ran cold within me. Something was wrong. Their expressions were somber as I ran up to them.

"What is it?" I called breathlessly. "What's happened?"

"'Tis your ma," Ian MacGreavy answered. He came to me and took my hand. "She's been hurt, Rose."

Gripped with fear, I broke loose from him and pushed past the others into the cottage. A few women from the coven were huddled around Ma's bed, stroking her hair and speaking in hushed tones. As I pressed closer, I saw Ma lying there, her eyes open but glazed. A pool of blood stained the blanket beneath her.

"Ma!" I knelt beside her, taking her hand. "What happened?"

Her face was a mask of pain, and from the look in her eyes I could see she was not completely in this world.

"She cannot speak," one of the elders told me. Mrs. Hazelton put her hand on my shoulder. "Seems that a stray hunter's arrow hit your ma. She was just leaving my cottage, having delivered a salve for my husband's breathing. She went down so fast! The huntsman never came forward, but I did hear his arrow whirring amidst the tree."

"I'll wager it was an arrow from a rival clan," Aislinn said, her face pinched with anger. "A deliberate act of aggression."

"We don't know that," Mrs. Hazelton pointed out.

I stood and looked over Ma's body. The arrow was still in her back. "This must be removed," I said, wondering how deep it had penetrated.

"But the heat in her body is high," said another elder who went by the name of Norn. She was a shriveled prune of a woman, but I had always been fond of her humor and her spirit. Norn touched Ma's forehead, clucking her tongue. "'Tis dangerous to take the arrow while she is feverish."

"Then we must take care of her fever." I pushed back my hair, then went to the basin to wash my hands. If there was ever an occasion that I needed to call upon the magick I had learned, this was it. I handed the broom to Aislinn to sweep the circle, then I went to Ma's Book of Shadows for remedies. "We need something to bring down the fever, and we must help her sleep. Removing the arrow might cause her great pain—it's better if she can rest." I leafed through the book. "I know we can start with chamomile and passionflowers."

"Anise in the tea will help her sleep," Norn told me. "And rosemary will help the pain."

"Add cayenne to stay the flow of blood," Mrs. Hazelton said.

I nodded as I leafed through the book. Finally I found a remedy for fever. "We'll need boneset in the tea to lower the fever," I said, rushing over to the jars and pouches to retrieve the herbs. "Pray Goddess that she's able to drink this at all!"

Norn had already put the kettle on the fire. Working together, we steeped a strong tea for Ma. As it brewed, I went to the altar and consecrated the tea and the comfrey poultice that Norn was preparing. I don't know what I said in the heated, dreadful moment, only that I summoned the Goddess to heal Her daughter and to work through my hands, and the others chanted, "So mote it be!"

We managed to prop my mother up so that the tea could pass over her lips. Still dazed, she sipped most of the contents. After that, her eyes closed and her breathing slowed.

"'Tis working," Norn said, dousing my mother's head with a cool cloth. "The fever is lifting."

Thanking the Goddess, I set to work on the arrow. I had to cut the skin a bit with my bolline to remove the barbed head, and as I worked, Ma's blood ran out steadily. At last the arrow was out, and I dressed the wound with the poultice and covered it with a clean white cloth.

"Now . . . she must rest," Norn said, her own voice cracking with weariness. "As should we. We'll know more when she awakens."

I lifted the plate containing the bloodied dressings and the arrow that I'd removed. Glancing down at the base, I noticed that it was marked with runes.

My body went cold as I deciphered their meaning. "Vykrothes . . ." So this was no hunting accident. The arrow was part of a spell cast by Siobhan, I was sure of it. Had not Mrs. Hazelton said that a hunter had never appeared? Surely a hunter would come forward to claim his prized deer or rabbit? No, this was not a normal arrow. It had been spelled by Siobhan.

Had she intended to hit me? I couldn't be sure. But one thing I was sure of: Siobhan had gone too far. She had to be stopped.

"A Vykrothe arrow . . ." Norn gasped.

"What?" Aislinn darted over to my side to study the arrow. "Oh, Goddess, this is truly war! To have our high priestess struck down by another clan!"

"It might have been an accident," Norn pointed out. "Come along now, Aislinn. You get yourself all liverish at every turn, girl!"

"Oh, some accident!" Aislinn exclaimed. "If it were not intended for Síle, why did the huntsman not come forward and state his mistake?"

"Quiet, girl!" Mrs. Hazelton hushed her. "You're loud enough to wake the dead, and Síle must sleep."

"Sleep, she will," Aislinn said in a quieter voice. "But when she awakens, she will find a changed world. A clan at war! For we cannot sit back and let our priestess be attacked!"

"Enough!" Placing a wrinkled hand on Aislinn's shoulder, Norn led her to the door. "Let us go so Síle can rest. Rose will watch over her." She ushered Aislinn out, then turned back to me. "You performed some powerful magick today," she told me softly, her eyes gleaming. "Your ma would be proud."

I nodded, my lips twisted with pain as the women filed out the door and returned to their own cottages. I closed the door and sighed, alone but for the quiet breathing of my mother in the bed. I cleaned up the bloodied things, dumped the old water, tidied the cottage, nursed Ma's head with a cool cloth. All the while I felt embittered and frightened.

I had brought a Vykrothe arrow upon my mother.

It was time for Siobhan to have a taste of her own evil.

Listlessly I paged through Ma's Book of Spells, praying for an answer. Aislinn was right. The Vykrothes deserved a taste of their own dark magick. But where do you begin if you've not been trained in the ways of darkness?

I turned to a spell called Death Drink and paused. I had never had much interest in this ritual. It called for a covener who wanted to visit their own mortality to drink a bitter brew. The potion sometimes made them a bit ill, but it was never fatal. As far as I was concerned, this was a tedious mind journey. So what if it led to inner wisdom?

But now, in this light, I wondered if I could use the death drink as a spell upon an unwilling victim . . . Siobhan.

I would add a few poisonous ingredients and a dark spell that would send Siobhan to death's door. She would not die, though she might wish she could. As I doused Ma's forehead with a cloth, I imagined Siobhan writhing in pain. Oh, I would send her a spell to end her viciousness.

"I'll need bitter ingredients," I whispered as I combed Ma's hair back with my fingers. "Cranberries from the bogs. Toadstools. And bitter essence of appleseeds."

Ma sighed contentedly, and I realized her fever had cooled. She slept soundly while I shuffled about the cottage, assembling herbs from our collection. When I was sure she was resting comfortably, with no sign of fever, I slipped out to consecrate the brew at my sacred circle.

Along the way I found a small wren hiding in the bushes. I paused, my life force pounding in my ears. I had never hurt one of the Goddess's creatures before, but everyone knew that the blood of a living animal made for potent dark magick. Quietly I knelt beside it, taking a large pouch from my belt. In the blink of an eye I swung the open pouch over the bird, trapping it with such deftness, I felt sure the Goddess intended it.

The stars were shrouded by clouds as I reached the clearing. I had expected darkness, with the new moon this eve. I squeezed the nectar from some sweet honeysuckles, thinking that if the potion tasted a bit palatable, Siobhan might drink it all. I added Siobhan's golden hair from her very own body. And much to my surprise, I barely flinched when it was time to cut the wren's neck and add its blood to the potion. There . . . the death drink was complete.

"Oh, Goddess," I whispered, "here I do display the chalice of death. Whoever drinks this shall journey to the land of darkness and dwell there until she comes to realize the error of her ways."

I dipped my athame in the chalice, then held the blade up to the sky. "A bitter potion to end a bitter evil!" I said. I placed a cloth over the chalice as drops began to fall from the sky. Cool, cleansing raindrops. From the distant hills came the rumble of thunder—the Goddess's answer. She had heard me. "So mote it be," I whispered.

The sun rose on a newly cleansed earth. I sat in bed, grateful that Síle was still resting comfortably. I arose and began to wash and dress. It was getting more and more difficult to find a place for my girdle between my belly and my breasts. Soon the world would know I was expecting a child. If all went well, I would have a husband before then.

I had just finished eating my breakfast of warm gruel and apples when Norn appeared at the cottage door, bearing a basket of biscuits.

"I have come to give you a rest from nursing your ma," she said, her beady eyes shining in her wrinkled face. "Go forth. You need some fresh air and release."

"Thank you," I said, taking a cloak to cover my belly and ward off the morning dew. "I have need of some time to commune with the Goddess," I told her. I started out the door, then turned back to retrieve the pitcher containing the death drink. "Let me not forget the ceremonial wine," I said.

"It is good that you are working your own spells," Norn told me. "Your mother must be pleased. Has she told you that you're likely to be our coven's next high priestess?"

"N-no," I said, surprised at her words. "But Ma has taught me well."

Norn smiled brightly as I headed down the path, on my way to Siobhan's cottage.

The trip to Lillipool had begun to seem shorter now that I'd traveled this way so oft of late. The sun was still low on the eastern hills when I rounded the hilltop near the heather fields. The MacMahon cottage sat in the sun, a young lad of five or six playing about near the woodpile beyond the house. He had long golden hair that hung to his shoulders and a smudge on his cheek. Probably Siobhan's younger brother, I wagered as I approached him. Perfect!

He was scalping the bark from various tree branches, his own unskilled attempts at carving figurines. When I drew close, he glanced up at me curiously. "Hark!" he said. "Do you come to visit me?"

"I come with a gift for Siobhan," I said, holding up the pitcher. "But since the hour is so early, I dare not disturb the household. Do you know her?" I asked.

"Aye! I am her brother Tysen." He eyed the pitcher curiously. "But what gift have you there?"

" 'Tis a sweet nectar from her love," I said. "Siobhan is to drink this first thing upon awakening." I lowered my voice, adding, "I think perhaps he has put a love spell upon it, hoping to capture your sister's heart. Do you know Diarmuid?"

He grinned. "Aye, I know him well. He owes me a ride upon his shoulders."

"I shall remind him of that," I said. Carefully I handed the pitcher to the boy. "Do you think you can handle a task of this magnitude?"

"Aye." He smiled proudly, his pale eyes gleaming. " 'Tis an easy task."

Tysen headed toward the house, and I headed back the way I had come with a new sense of righteousness and balance. Siobhan had struck down my mother, but her evil magick was now cycling back to her.

When I returned to the cottage, Ma was sitting up and eating biscuits with Norn.

"Look who's feeling better," Norn said, all smiles as she took the kettle of tea off the fire. "That's some powerful magick you wrought yesterday, Rose. Síle, your daughter is truly blessed by the Goddess."

"Indeed," my mother said. "I have always admired her powers. I am fortunate she was at hand yesterday when I was in dire need of them."

I thanked Norn for her help, and she insisted on leaving the biscuits behind. After she departed, Ma moved back to the bed to drink her tea.

"What a world of difference," I told her as I sat at the table. I bit into a biscuit and brushed flour from my fingers. "You look so much better."

"Thanks to you," she said. "You have come a long way in your magick, Rose."

I smiled. Perhaps Ma finally realized that I'd been working hard to learn the ways of the Goddess.

Ma sipped her tea, then let her head drop back. "But I must say, my mind traveled to some frightening places in my dreams. I saw you concocting a dark spell, inviting in evil, conjuring a potion with the intention to hurt someone. I saw your athame raised to dark thunderclouds and—did it rain last night?"

"I think it did," I said innocently. The biscuit was now wedged in my throat, and I no longer had the appetite for it. Ma's insightfulness scared me. It was difficult to fool a high priestess—especially if she was your mother!

"Such frightening visions," Ma said.

Brushing off my hands, I went to my mother's bedside. "Shall I change the dressing or wait?"

"Let it wait," Ma said, lifting the cloth to show me the wound. "It seems to be healing."

I nodded. "It does look much better. But you should sleep. You need to heal."

"I will, though I fear my sleep will be haunted by more of the same dreams."

"'Twas but a vision of your delirium," I assured her. "Now that you have no fever, your dreams will be gentle."

Síle smiled. "Advice from my daughter?"

I nodded. "Sage advice."

12.

Reversing a Spell

While Ma slept, I went down to wash at the brook, trying to think of a way to sneak off and see Diarmuid. I could not abandon Ma in her current state, not for a long period. And although I was grateful that she was healing quickly, my patience was wearing thin.

"You need your da," I said, rubbing my belly as I waded in the cool shallows.

I would have to give Ma one more day. After that, perhaps I could convince Kyra or Norn to stay with her while I went to fetch the man who would become my husband.

Feeling cleansed and refreshed, I headed back to the cottage. When I came upon the main road, I spied Kyra tramping along, a basket on her arm.

"I have sweet oat cakes for your ma," she said, "and dreadful news for you." She took my hand and pulled me off the road. "Did you cast a spell over Siobhan? Some kind of deadly potion?"

"I did." I squared my shoulders. "After what she did to my mother, I—"

"I'm not blaming you," Kyra interrupted, "but rumor has it that Siobhan's younger brother has fallen ill. The boy seems to have a sleeping sickness, his breathing slowed to frightening depths, his body racked by convulsions."

I gasped. "He drank the potion?"

Kyra nodded sadly. "The poor little thing."

I thought of Tysen, carving the bark diligently. The way he had been so proud to bear the pitcher to his sister. I'd had no idea he would drink it himself. But then, he was only a child—perhaps a mischievous one. I should have realized that when I handed him the death drink. I bit my lower lip, wondering if all of the death drink had gone to the wrong person. "And how is Siobhan?" I asked, hoping that she might have had a few sips herself.

"In a fury," Kyra answered. "Siobhan is telling everyone that the potion was spelled, an evil spell cast by you!"

I folded my arms defensively. "The cup was not marked, and no one saw me give it to Tysen." At least, I didn't think anyone saw me. "Siobhan will never be able to prove her suspicions," I said.

"Perhaps not," Kyra agreed. "Still, 'tis a sad thing to see sickness in one so young."

"Indeed." With every ounce of my might I wished that I could take back the spell—take it all back and restore Tysen's good health. Perhaps I could.

But I didn't want to involve Kyra in this, especially now that I had dabbled in dark magick. I thanked her for the cakes and headed back to the cottage, thinking of possible spells. There was a spell intended to undo the original spell—certainly worth a try. And there was an endless variety of healing spells. Surely any combination of those would cure the boy.

Back at the cottage, Ma was asleep. I checked her for

fever, then sat at the table with her Book of Shadows. After much searching I found the spell of reversal:

> *On the eve of the new moon I cast a spell,*
> *And the effects I created, I must now quell.*
> *May this spell be lifted and I now gifted with . . .*

"With good health for Tysen," I whispered aloud.

The spell called for protective stones such as amethyst or smokey quartz, and I was to use one white and one black candle for balance. I bit my lips, determined to sneak out to my sacred place in the woods as soon as night fell and save Tysen. For now I could only assemble the things I would need.

Night had fallen. Ma had been to the table to eat, but now she was back in bed again, too weak to stay up for long. Still, she was healing well. I had cleaned and dressed her wound, and it was starting to close with no redness or discharge. I was grateful that she would recover.

She dozed upon her pillow now, and I was ready to slip out and reverse the spell that had befallen poor Tysen. My tools and herbs were assembled. All that I needed was a gemstone from Ma's cupboard. I opened the cabinet door and poked about, searching for a stone with the right charge. I found a malachite, a bluish stone with bands of white. Holding it thoughtfully in my hands, I realized it would be a good stone to keep near me. Malachite was known to give wisdom, pointing one in the right direction, giving guidance. I was about to slip it in my pocket when the stone broke in half! Part of it tumbled from my hand, falling to the table with a thud.

Ma bolted up in bed. "What was that?" she asked.

"This malachite," I told her, picking up the pieces from the floor. "It broke in two!"

"Oh, dear Goddess!" Ma exclaimed. She tried to rise from her bed, but I could see that the movement drained her.

"Don't get up, Ma," I said, tucking the blanket over her. "It's all right."

"But it's not! This has dire meaning. Malachite breaks in two to give you a warning of danger. Something terrible is going to happen, Rose!"

I swallowed hard, trying to hold back my own panic. *Oh, Goddess, are my dark spells coming back to me?* I couldn't bear to tell Ma the truth of my worries, to admit how deep I had fallen into spells she didn't approve of.

"Oh, then . . . it must have been predicting your accident with the arrow," I said, turning my face to the cupboard. I put the two pieces of malachite back on the shelf. "Because, actually, the stone broke last week. I simply forgot to mention it to you."

"It was already broken?"

I could feel her fear draining away.

"Well, then, let's hope you are right. Perhaps you are." She turned on her side, content to fall back asleep.

I found an amethyst in her collection, then collected the candles and herbs I had gathered. It was time to save Tysen.

Quietly I slipped out the door and started up the path. Ahead of me light spilled down the lane. What was it from? A moment later torches floated up the path, heading this way.

I recoiled in fear. What had happened? Had Tysen died already and the Vykrothes come to punish me? I backed up to the door and nearly fell inside. Ma was already up, hobbling toward me.

"What is it, Rose?" she asked in a hoarse voice. "I sense the danger. What's happening?"

"A band of people is coming," I said, rushing to stow away the things I had collected for my spell. "I don't know who they are, but they are not Vykrothes."

"Let us see," Ma said, shuffling painfully to the door.

I followed her out to the sea of darkness bobbing with torches and ghostly faces. In the lead the village reverend stepped forward, his mouth a slash of contempt.

"What business do you have with us so late at night, Reverend Winthrop?" my mother asked politely. "Have you come to pay a call upon the sick, for that is what I am. A victim of a hunter's arrow."

"I am sorry for your hardship," Reverend Winthrop said. "But I am here on a mission from the Almighty Father. I have come to take your daughter to prison, Síle. On the morrow she will be tried as a witch."

"It cannot be!" my mother protested.

"No!" I cried. I clutched my belly, buckling to my knees. A witch! How could it be that these people knew of my love for the Goddess? I had moved stealthily, attending church on Sundays and always careful not to speak of my true life around the villagers. A coldness overcame me as I stared out at them, my tears blurring their faces.

How could it be?

"Upon whose order do you take her?" my mother demanded.

The reverend did not answer. But someone stepped forward from the crowd—Siobhan!

"Upon my word!" she shouted. "I know her to be a witch, and I will testify against her."

"No!" I pleaded. "'Tis not fair. She hates me! She wants to have revenge!"

But no one seemed to hear my cries as the men stepped forward and grabbed me by the shoulders. Brusquely they bound my wrists behind me and shoved me away from the cottage.

"No!" I cried, turning back to see Ma huddled at the door-way. "Ma! Please!"

But she merely watched me go with a stricken expression on her face. She held out a hand to me, as if I could clasp on and save myself from drowning.

But I could not. I marched off to prison, my heart hammering with fear that this was truly my death march. Because of Siobhan, I had been named as a witch. And no one, no one in the Highlands, had ever faced those charges and escaped alive.

On the morning of my trial a guard woke me and roughly ushered me into a cottage near the village center. I hoped they were bringing me to the table to break my fast, but when I saw the minister, Reverend Winthrop, along with a stout, bearded man, I reared back in fear.

"Dr. Wellington is here to examine you for the mark of the devil, Rose MacEwan," said the reverend. "Off with your gown."

The guard at the door crossed his arms, smiling at me.

I had never been ashamed of my body, having been raised among circles of unclad witches, but to go naked before such hostile eyes. . . . I began to tremble. Would he realize that I was with child? If he did, 'twould prejudice the town against me.

"I cannot," I said, folding my arms across my chest protectively.

"Balderdash!" the reverend shouted. He stepped forward and tore at the collar of my gown. "Remove your clothes, and I'll remind you to make haste, for your trial is upon us."

"No!" I shrieked, trying to pull away from him. I felt like a trapped animal; there was no way out. Closing my eyes, I began to take off my gown.

I stood there naked, feeling their lust and hatred swirl around me. Something jabbed at my buttocks, and I opened my eyes to see the physician jabbing at me with a stick, as if I were chattel in a field. Keeping his distance, he touched my buttocks, my thighs, my belly, my breasts. Humiliation burned in my throat, and I closed my eyes again.

I could not tell whether he knew I was with child. At this point the mound at my belly was quite pronounced and my breasts were swollen with milk, but I wasn't sure this physician knew the realities of a woman's body. His examination seemed more motivated by lust than professional interest.

And thus I began the day of my trial, naked before three peculiar men. After that I was allowed to dress and given a bowl of gruel, which I gobbled up eagerly. It was not enough food to sustain my babe, and I wondered if there would be more at lunch.

After breakfast I was dragged out to the center of our village, where I was tied rather barbarically to a hitching post. Villagers were free to assemble around me and witness the nightmare, and most of the villagers I saw every Sunday in church were in attendance. Among the faces gathered there, I saw the members of our coven—the MacGreavys, Norn, Aislinn, and the others. Ma was there, leaning gingerly on

Miller MacGreavy's cart. I spied Meara with two of the little ones in tow, and I wondered if she was their ma now. Kyra and Falkner were conspicuously absent, but I suspected that their parents had been fearful for their safety. If the village reverend started to get greedy, he might look for others who were guilty by association.

Standing in the center of the village, sweating under the late August sun and the scrutiny of so-called holy men, I felt horribly exposed. An alarming odor filled the air, something I could not identify. Was it a burning herb?

No, I thought, swallowing against the biting taste in my throat. It's the smell of fear. My fear.

Reverend Winthrop began talking to the crowd, telling of evils prevailing amongst us. I was trying to listen, trying to create a defense in my mind when I saw someone moving through the crowd—a lean, solid figure.

Diarmuid!

I felt my life force rising as he turned toward me. Our eyes locked, and I could feel it in the air between us. He still loved me. He had come to tell me that and to free me from these charges. He would come forward during the trial and rescue me. I closed my eyes and focused on sending him a message. Diarmuid would rescue me once again. This would all be over soon.

You've come to save me! I told him in a tua labra. *I knew you would come for me.*

I waited for an answer.

But all I heard was the voice of the reverend accusing me of being a witch. "Coming upon her at the brook one morning, I saw her conducting what must certainly be a pagan ritual," he said in his whiny voice.

I suddenly recalled the morning when I'd heard someone on the path. The morning after Beltane, when I'd slipped off my clothes for a thorough cleansing . . .

"I was washing," I said, looking out at the crowd for validation. "Do not most maidens bathe upon rising?"

"Without a stitch of clothing?" Reverend Winthrop asked.

A few of the Presbyterians snickered, as if he'd made a coarse joke.

"Why do you laugh, when most of you could use a thorough cleansing in the river?" Ma said, standing tall. The crowd grew silent. "Or is that odor the stench of hysteria? For I have yet to see a person so accused treated fairly in these Highlands."

The minister folded his arms, appraising my mother. "Woman, what is your claim here? This is a formal inquisition."

"I am the mother of Rose MacEwan, and I know her to be a kind and noble child," Síle said. Her hair was covered by a modest veil, her voice filled with a fortitude that belied her injury. "Whatever evil you have charged her with is false, I swear a solemn oath to that. And I charge you to release her and return her to her proper home."

It was dangerous for anyone to speak in my defense, but Ma had been willing to take that chance. In some ways, I knew I didn't deserve it. Pressing one hand against the child in my belly, I marveled at how deep a mother's love could run.

Reverend Winthrop puckered his lips, as if Síle's words had left a sour taste in his mouth. "These are the words of her mother," he announced formally. "Although I've yet to know a mother who clearly sees her child's true flaws."

I turned to Diarmuid and sent him an urgent message: *The man shows disrespect toward my mother!* I wanted to say. *Step forward and set him aright!* But now he was watching the reverend, pretending not to understand me.

"So," the minister went on, "it was no surprise when this young maiden came to me with proof that Rose MacEwan is a witch." He gestured toward Siobhan. "Tell us what you know, please."

Siobhan stepped forward, her long neck craning as she lifted her chin proudly. "She is a witch!" she said in a tinny voice. "I have witnessed her performing her craft."

Although she was hardly convincing, she smiled gleefully.

I turned to Diarmuid, wondering what he thought of his betrothed now. Had he known that she was a backstabbing hypocrite?

Diarmuid's face was pale, his blue eyes flashing with something I couldn't determine. Surprise? Perhaps he hadn't heard that Siobhan was my chief accuser.

Step forward and make her cease, I ordered him. *You have the power to stop her. . . . Don't let this drag on!*

But he didn't seem to be receiving my messages. Where was his mind today?

"What have you seen Rose MacEwan doing?" Reverend Winthrop prodded Siobhan. "Remember what you told me?"

"Aye!" Siobhan answered. "I have seen her dancing in the woods at night! Dancing with the devil!"

Her words lashed out like the crack of a whip. How could she say that? Even if she hated me, did she not realize those words would be my death sentence? I pressed my hands to my hot cheeks, too afraid to respond, too frightened to cry.

The crowd gasped and murmured.

"Quiet, please!" the reverend shouted. "Let's not waver from the point at hand. Did you or did you not see Rose

MacEwan in her dance with Satan?" he asked Siobhan.

"I did!" she shouted. "And I can prove it." She pointed a finger at me, hatred gleaming in her pale gray eyes. "Rose MacEwan is with child! She is carrying the devil's spawn!"

I felt stung. How did she know I was with child? Had Diarmuid told her? It would have been a huge betrayal, something I could not believe of him. She must have found out some other way. But how?

The crowd was rumbling with speculation. Ma had collapsed onto Miller MacGreavy's cart, and I saw Norn embrace her. I tried to catch Diarmuid's eye, but he was blocked by one of the villagers, who was laughing heartily. Should I send him another tua labra, or was that a waste of time? *Oh, Goddess, help me!*

"Is it true, Dr. Wellington?" Reverend Winthrop asked the physician. "Is Rose MacEwan with child?"

Dr. Wellington stroked his bristly beard as if the answer lay there in the folds of his chin. "Well, aye, 'tis true."

"My child is not the devil's spawn," I cried. "She is a healthy, human child with a father who will love her!"

"Liar!" Siobhan shouted. "There is no father! Rose MacEwan has lain with the devil. That is why her belly is swollen with his evil seed!"

Reverend Winthrop made the sign of the cross, and those standing closest to me took a step back, as if my evil could spread to them.

"There is a father for my child!" I insisted. "He is among us now." I dared not name him, for fear that the crowd would turn on him, too. The answer had to come from him; Diarmuid had to be the one to stand up and lay claim to me as his future bride and mother of his child. By doing so he could turn this scandalous dilemma into something honorable in the eyes of the Christians, who at least believed in redemption.

I glanced toward him, beseeching him, but he did not move. What was he waiting for? *I need you—now! It's time for you to save me. Denounce Siobhan's lie. Claim me as your own true love and lover.*

"A father among us?" Reverend Winthrop said tartly. He glanced over his shoulders at the men in the crowd. "All right, then. Let the father of Rose MacEwan's child step forward. What human among us has lain with this woman?"

I looked at Diarmuid, begging him to act now.

But he would not meet my glance. It was as if he were cast in stone, a useless pillar of rock.

Please! I thought, beseeching him with every fiber of my being. *Please . . . they're going to kill me and our baby!*

But he did not move.

"Oh, Goddess," I mumbled under my breath. "Let it not be. He is choosing her! He is choosing her over me!"

"Just as I suspected." The reverend shook his head, eyeing me with mock sadness. "There is no father, is there?" His eyes glittered with malice.

"There is!" I insisted.

He swung out a hand and struck me across the face. The blow was so sudden that I felt blinded for a second. "Your lies shall not be tolerated here. I had hoped you would accept the grace of the Lord and make a confession; however, I see that repentance is not forthcoming. It is the demon in you, and I fear you are too far gone for redemption."

I wanted to protest, but my throat had gone dry.

Going over to a horse trough, Reverend Winthrop pushed

back the sleeves of his gown, making a show of washing his hands. "I wash my hands of the matter of your redemption. I do believe you are guilty as charged."

"Aye, she is guilty!" someone cried.

"Guilty! Guilty!" The cry became a chant taken up by the villagers around me.

I felt myself collapsing against the hitching post, my hands hugging my belly. I couldn't let them hurt my babe. But how could I stop the swell of hatred that raged out of control?

"Guilty! Guilty! Guilty!"

Strong arms clamped around me. I felt myself being lifted, then dragged off through the crowd. Villagers stared at me, their eyes full of scorn or pity or curiosity. One woman snatched her children away and tucked them behind her skirts, as if I would harm them. How wrong she was. Didn't she know I would defend any child, especially my own, to the ends of time?

"Another useless Wodebayne to the gallows," I heard a Vykrothe man mutter just loud enough for me to hear. "'Tis no loss for us."

Is that what all of this had boiled down to? Hatred and prejudice? I wondered, but my thoughts were clouded with pain and confusion.

"At last she'll be getting what she deserves," said a familiar voice.

I glanced up to see Siobhan sidling up to Diarmuid, a smug expression on her face. Beside her Diarmuid stood staring at the ground.

Not man enough to defend me! I wanted to say, but the words were caught in the painful lump lodged in my throat.

I dug my heels into the ground, making the guards halt for a moment. "Mark my words, Siobhan," I told her, my voice crack-ing with emotion. "Your evil will come back to you threefold!"

"Begone!" she said, waggling her fingers at me like a sprite. "You'll not harm me again."

Without thought I was upon her, grabbing and scraping in an attempt to shatter her silly composure. I felt my nails dig into her skin, scratching the side of her cheek.

"Aaah!" she yelped. "The witch has attacked me again!"

The men quickly yanked me off her, but before they dragged me away, I had the satisfaction of seeing her sad little pout, along with a trickle of blood running down her graceful neck.

That is the neck that should be snapped at the gallows! I wanted to scream. She had tried to kill my mother, had she not? The urge to send dealan-dé her way was strong, and it took all my restraint to control myself as the men took me off to my tiny prison.

My cell was actually the springhouse behind a villager's cot-tage. The roof was made of leaky straw thatching, but the mud-plastered stone walls prevented my escape. Tossed onto the dirt floor there, I curled into a ball and thought of Diarmuid, my heart truly breaking. What had happened to the power of our love?

He had said that I was destined for great things—to become high priestess! And he knew the Goddess's plan for our union—that together we could unite all the clans!

But no. The path to redemption had been crossed by Siobhan, and Diarmuid had succumbed to her. He had failed me, failed us, failed our child.

Oh, Goddess, how could he be so disloyal? Disappointment overwhelmed me as I fell into a dark state, my hand resting upon the child within my belly.

13.

A Spell for the Darkest Hour

The creak of a door. A sliver of light.

Someone was entering my chamber.

"Hark!" he said, peering over the flame of the candle.

I sat up on the dirt floor. "Diarmuid?" My head was clogged from sleep, but indeed it was him, coming into the cell.

"Where are the guards?" I asked in surprise.

"They are blind to me," he said as the door creaked closed behind him. "I cast a see-me-not spell, rather successfully, I might add. And those bumblers are spelled deep asleep."

How could he joke at a time like this? I turned my face away, not willing to meet his eyes. "Have you come to gloat over my demise?" I asked.

"Of course not. I've come to extract one last promise. I was pleased by the way you held your tongue today, not mentioning my name. I trust you'll keep silent till the end."

I spun around to glare at him. "Silent!" I shouted. "Silence is the reason I am here! Why did you not answer my messages?"

I stamped the ground with my foot. "Why did you not come forward to defend me and claim your child?"

He lowered his chin, his blue eyes abrasive. "How am I to know the bairn is mine?"

Furious, I took a swing at him, but he bobbed so that my fist caught only air. As I stumbled back, he caught my arms and held me in place. His eyes swept down my body to my breasts, my swollen belly. "And you thought I would claim your child?" he said with sudden disdain. "Knowing your wanton ways, you've probably bedded dozens like me."

His words infuriated me, but my fury was checked by my revelation. The man standing before me was not noble nor true nor even kind. And he had never been the sweet perfection I'd glimpsed under the Goddess's sky.

His pentagram dangled at his neck, glinting mockingly.

Suddenly I wanted to scratch out his glittering eyes and smite the grin from his pretty face. I did not love this man. How had I ever loved one who so cagily used me, took of my body and my heart, then abandoned me for dead?

"Get out!" I growled. I kicked at his legs, aiming high but just glancing off the top of his thigh.

Still, it was enough to scare him off. He released my hands as he doubled over.

Reaching out, I grabbed at his pentagram and pulled. He did not deserve to wear this! He did not deserve to pay homage to the Goddess! He made a little choking sound as it snapped off. With a feeling of righteousness I dropped the pentagram to the ground.

Diarmuid rubbed his neck. "You're rather feisty for a condemned woman," he said. "And I should be the one throwing punches, what with the way you charmed me. I found the rose stone in your pocket. Powerful magick you make. 'Twas lovely while it lasted, but love soon fades to lust and needs. And my needs are well fulfilled by my own coven."

Fury burned inside me. "And Siobhan," I said. "You have lain with her because . . . because 'tis the easiest path to take."

He shrugged. "A man has certain obligations to his clan, and to marry a Wodebayne, I would have been falling short of everyone's expectations. You truly caught my eye. Even when Siobhan undid the power of your charmed stone, my desire to take you did not abate. Even now . . . I long to hold you one last time. . . ." He reached for me hungrily.

"In a pig's eye!" I shouted, pushing him away. "Begone from here, Diarmuid! For our passion was not about lust nor favor! Did you not stand in the circle with me and summon the Goddess? Did we not pledge our love under her sky and promise to—"

"A witch says many things, chants many things," he said. "Often we say words we do not comprehend. 'Tis part of the—"

"I knew what I was saying!" Hatred swelled within me as all illusions of beauty and goodness melted away from him, revealing a diabolical monster. I pointed to the door. "Begone from here before I have at you, for I swear, I will tear the hair from your lovely head."

"Don't you threaten me, Rose!" Diarmuid lunged at me, backing me against the wall. "For despite your powers with the Goddess, I have the physical power to overcome you." His eyes sparkled deviously. I felt stunned, unable to move. Was it possible that this boy—this boy I had seen as the answer to all of my prayers—would ravish me by force?

I struggled to get away, but he only tightened his grip.

"I will have you, Rose, for who will stop me? You are locked in prison, completely alone. Do you think the guards will answer your cries? The pleas of a witch sentenced to die?" He pushed me into the cold stone wall.

I felt sickened by his touch, furious at his determination to overcome me. And I had loved him! How had I ever loved this cruel, conniving beast? Feeling it was hopeless to fight him, I collapsed against the wall. He was stronger than I. I knew I had to summon magick, but my mind was wild and scattered.

Seeing me relax, he released my hands and lifted my skirts. "Come on, Rose," he said. "It'll be worse if you fight me."

Seizing the freedom of my hands, I grasped his face and pressed my nails in, hoping to scratch his pretty blue eyes out.

He gasped as my fingers penetrated his skin. His hands quickly encircled my wrists and pried me off, but not before I'd managed to scratch his cheeks. "Are you mad?"

"So they say!" I wrenched my hands free of him and backed away, rubbing my wrists. "But I'll not spend my last night on earth being defiled by the lust of a lying coward."

He pressed his fingers to his cheek and saw the crimson smear there. "You drew blood," he said in horror. For a moment I thought he would weep with despair.

Focusing my mind, I held up my hands to ward him off. "Next time I'll use dealan-dé," I told him. "And if I had an athame, I would plunge it right through your festering heart."

Holding a hand against his cheek, he sucked in his breath. "I cannot wait till the morrow." His face was hollow and angular in the candlelight, a hideous, hateful specter. "I will relish the moment of your death."

Before I could respond, he fled from the cell, leaving only a lit candle behind.

A lit candle. Fire of the Goddess.

Diarmuid had left behind the one element I needed to balance out my circle. I had earth, wind, water, air . . . and now, despite all the attempts of the guards to keep it away from me, I had fire.

My fists clenched, I stared at the flame as fury raged within me. I burned for all the Wodebaynes who had suffered injustice at the hands of rival witches. Fire raged within me for Diarmuid—not the fires of passion, but the fires of hatred and fury. I burned with vengeance for Siobhan, who had stolen my place as Diarmuid's wife and sentenced me to death, who had tried to take my mother's life, too. And above all I was afire with love and sorrow for the babe in my belly, the child who had been condemned before she'd had a chance to take her first breath.

Sweat beaded on my forehead and dripped down my neck. What was happening? Pressing my hands to my cheeks, I found that my skin was sizzling hot to the touch, feverish despite the cool night air.

A fire raged within me, a fire from the Goddess, and I realized she was summoning me to a mystickal destiny. *What?* I asked. *Where shall I go? Which way to turn?* I felt pent up and trapped, unable to commune with her. I needed to see the moon.

Glancing up at the thatched roof, I realized that I could prob- ably reach it with the help of the one chair in my prison. I pulled the chair to the highest spot and climbed up. Aye, my fingertips pressed against the thatching. I pulled at the straw, tugging it loose. I would claw and scrape until my fingers bled if it meant reaching out to the Goddess on my last night upon this earth.

As I plucked at the straw, I thought of my purpose. I could not see my way to escape from my death or to save my child. But what of my legacy . . . my destiny before the Goddess? Would I be known only as a young witch who had feuded with a Vykrothe girl?

I recalled what my mother had said about Da, about his feud with the Vykrothes. Now, so many years later, I had become entangled with the same clan. Was that part of the Goddess's plan? Perhaps my very purpose was to dismantle the Vykrothes' power once and for all. I could not actively go after Siobhan, but I could place a curse upon her from behind these prison walls. One last spell, one final wave of revenge before she had me killed.

Bit by bit, the straw tumbled down to the earth. Then I yanked on a thick piece, and a fat section of thatching fell to the floor of the stone hut, making a crumbling sound that might have been heard by the guard if he had not been still asleep and snoring thanks to Diarmuid's spell. When the dust cleared, I was gazing upon a dark patch of sky with a virgin crescent moon.

I came down from the chair and stood, arms up, in the sliver of pale moonlight. 'Twas but a dim patch, but I could feel its power lifting me to the sky. I no longer felt trapped. I was communing with the Goddess, opening myself up to my own destiny.

The air seemed to crackle with magick as I held my hands open to the Goddess. "Show me the tools and how to use them," I begged.

In the candlelight the tips of my fingernails seemed black. Examining them, I realized it was blood. Blood and skin scraped from Siobhan and Diarmuid. 'Twas a powerful beginning, to have a piece of their body to place upon my makeshift altar. I scraped the dried crust from under my nails and placed it carefully on a clean tin plate left to me by the guards.

Staring at the scraps of Diarmuid and Siobhan, I began to feel the way clearly. 'Twas the Goddess's will, this spell, and she lit my path.

"Sweep the circle," came the Goddess's voice. Or was I remembering Ma's voice from one of the coven circles? "Sweep . . . sweep," it called out to me, stirring my powers.

I gathered straw from my sleeping pallet and wove it into a small broom, which I used to sweep a circle inside the springhouse. Then I lit my makeshift broom afire and swept my circle with flames. The smoke burned my throat, but I breathed it gladly, wanting to cense my hair and skin with this powerful spell. Finally I left the broom to burn in the center and turned to the candle.

Carefully, so as not to extinguish the flame, I carved runes into the single candle that Diarmuid had brought. I spelled out the Vykrothe name, then wrote the runes for death beside it. Then I added runes for Diarmuid's name, for truly he deserved the wrath of the Goddess for his betrayal of Her, his betrayal of me and my child.

As I set the candle down, I noticed Diarmuid's pentagram on the ground. I picked up the gold coin and blew off the dust. 'Twould make a fine brand upon my body. If I was to go to the gallows, I would want to have the mark of the Goddess upon me and my child.

I built up the center fire with twigs and straw of the thatching. Blowing on the flames until the embers glowed, I knew what I had to do.

A spell to put an end to treachery.

A spell to destroy Siobhan and Diarmuid. To punish their evil. Mayhap this was the Goddess's will for me—my destiny.

A spell to set the balance among the clans aright once again.

Casting Diarmuid's pentagram into the flames, I felt the fever within me rise. Gasping, I threw back my head and cast my eyes upon the crescent in the sky. The fire within me was raging, my skin dripping, my cheeks burning. I slipped off my gown and stood naked in the square of light.

"I draw the power of generations of Wodebaynes into myself, merging with her power, the pure essence of the Goddess."

Gazing down into the crusty blood, I said: "I have cast this circle to perform the act of vengeance that the Vykrothes have truly earned. I place a curse upon their feet, that they may stumble along the path of light and fall into darkness. Cursed be their wombs, that they shall fail to produce new offspring. Cursed be their warmongering hearts, that they will no longer beat steady and true. Cursed be their sight, that they shall never again see through the Goddess's veil to her true beauty."

Holding the tin of blood over the flame, I charged it with fire, saying: "As Siobhan lit a fire of hatred in this world, so shall her blood boil. Send her own malice, greed, and wickedness back to her—threefold!" I tossed the dried blood into the fire, and a sizzling sound issued forth. I imagined leagues of tabihs—a huge wave of them—rising up and sweeping over Siobhan's pretty flaxen head. Black droplets of pain rained down upon Diarmuid, staining his sparkling blue eyes, burning his hair, sinking into his lovely cheeks. The black spells danced over them, blocking out all light until their bodies were a dissolving mass of darkness.

"This offering is for you, Goddess," I said. "Cast your hatred upon the head of Siobhan and her Vykrothe family. Cast darkness upon Diarmuid and his cruel family. And if you have no evil to send, I summon the fallen angels, arbiters of evil! Use my powers to mete out this justice!"

The powers of darkness swirled around me. I felt buffeted by smoky darkness, mired in the pain and suffering that I was sending from my heart to the hearts of mine enemies.

Using a thick piece of straw, I fished Diarmuid's pentagram out of the fire. I thought of the way Diarmuid had drawn pentagrams in the air . . . the foolish boy. His magick was so weak!

The pentagram had turned black with heat, but I reached for it. 'Twas time to brand myself to the ways of the Goddess, despite the pain.

My fingertips singed as I picked it up, but the pain seemed cool against the fire that raged inside me. Pressing the pentagram to my belly, I charged each point of the star.

"I summon the powers of earth," I whispered hoarsely, "wind, water, fire, and spirit." Pain brought tears to my eyes, but it seemed minor in comparison to the pain that filled me. The pain of losing my baby, of losing my life and love.

My pain must not go unpunished!

Kneeling before the fire, I imagined the wave of evil surrounding Siobhan, sucking her in, slamming her, crashing over her helpless body and swallowing the other cruel Vykrothes in its wake.

"I cast this spell for my baby," I said. "For myself, and for every other Wodebayne who has ever been wronged. Goddess, sweep over the treacherous ones and let their own evil be compounded!" I felt a surge of power, a wave that drew me up, thrumming around me, buoying my body above the chaotic forces at work. I was rising up, hovering above my cell, above my own village and Ma's cottage, above the Highlands. Beneath me were the soft greens of summer fields, the crisp dark crown of woodlands, the silver blue of lochs with the cool mist of evening rising up from them.

Wondering what held me suspended, I looked down and saw a wave of pure darkness. I was riding a crescent of black, a coursing molten liquid wrought of the blood of dead Wodebaynes, of my father and his father, of Fionnula and other tormented clan members. 'Twas my blood and my child's blood, raging and thrashing over the Highlands—a river of evil crashing into the village of Lillipool.

Then, all at once, I was released.

I collapsed to the ground, weak and spent. I slipped into a dream state, feeling fires raging around me. Was my cell burning? Had I remembered to douse the burning broom?

I wasn't sure, but I could not summon the strength to lift myself from the floor. If I were destined to die now, perhaps it was better at my own hand than at the hands of the villagers. What was to come at the end of this life? I remembered Ma speaking of death being rebirth . . . the Wheel turns and we move on to a new life. Would I find my baby in that new world? I hugged my belly, feeling the child kick. "I will be there for you," I whispered tearfully. "I will be there."

*   *   *

I am riding upon his shoulders at the seashore. Then suddenly we are here in the town square, dancing with torches like witches around the Beltane fires. Then I am on a seaside cliff, holding a soft

bundle in my arms. When I open the flap, I peer into the face of
my own baby. A girl, of course. She smells of honeysuckle and clover.
But we cannot stay here. The ocean is rising from a storm. And
suddenly the wave is cresting, taller and taller, over our heads. I must
run to save her. . . .

I lifted my head and reached forward, trying to grasp my
baby. My fingers brushed the ashes of my ceremonial fire, and I
remembered that I was in my cell, sleeping in my circle under
a smoky gray sky.

I arose and slipped on my gown, struggling to fasten the
girdle over my bulging belly. Throughout the night the shouts
of villagers and the noise of people scrambling about had penetrated the numbness that gripped me. Now that daylight was
flooding in through the ceiling, the smell of fire was thick in
the air. How could the smoke from my spell linger so?

The door opened, and a bowl of biscuits was tossed in.
"Here's your milk," the guard said, eyeing me warily as he
placed the pitcher inside the door. "And don't be laying a
curse upon my head, for I am just doing my job, and I have
three young bairns at home."

I blinked. What was he blubbering about? But before I
could ask, the door slammed shut, leaving me to my breakfast. I
ate every last crumb, surprised at the calm that had overtaken
me. I had resigned myself that my baby and I would be reborn
together; that was the vision I would cling to in my last hours.

When the door opened for me to go to the gallows, I
stepped into the smoky haze with my chin high and a small
measure of courage. If Siobhan and the others were going to
condemn me, I would not let them have the satisfaction of
seeing that they had indeed broken my spirit.

I will see you when the Wheel turns, I told the child within me. How I will delight in the sight of your sweet face!

I followed the guards to the gallows, surprised that they did not try to bind my hands or manhandle me today. They did cast nervous glances, but somehow their eyes no longer held the utter disdain I'd seen the day before.

Arriving at the village square, I was surprised to see such a small group of witnesses assembled. I wondered at the scarcity of onlookers, especially when I had been such a spectacle the day before. And where was Ma? I couldn't believe she wouldn't come to be with me as I took my last breath. Kyra stood by the gallows, swathed in black. But Diarmuid and Siobhan were absent, as was the village reverend, who had been my chief persecutor.

I looked at the strange faces, wondering what had happened to my enemies. Had the spell worked? Perhaps Siobhan had been stricken down, unable to attend my execution. The thought offered some satisfaction.

As I walked up to the gallows, Kyra came up to me. "If I may have a moment," she told the guards, and they stepped back. Kyra put her arms around me for a hug, and I wanted to cry, feeling as if she were the last person on earth who cared for me. I hugged her back, the sting of tears in my eyes.

"You shouldn't be doing this," I told her, my voice cracking with emotion. "They'll persecute you just for knowing me."

"I have lied to them, Rose, and they remember me not," she whispered in my ear. "As I stand here, the guards think I'm a preacher's daughter from a village to the north, come to speak the word of the Christian god to a condemned prisoner."

I sobbed, afraid to let her go.

"Don't look down," she whispered, "but I'm pressing a charm into your hands for protection. Amber. I charged it myself." She winced, adding, "I hope it works."

"Thank you," I whispered, pleased that Kyra was working her own magick at last. "You are the only one who's come to say good-bye."

"Many did not survive the night." She frowned. "It seems there was a terrible fire in Lillipool last night. That is why smoke hangs in the air."

"A fire?" I tried to tamp down my curiosity. What had my spell done?

Kyra nodded. "Nobody was present to see the flames, only the ruin left in its wake. It appears that it swept through the village, then leaped to neighboring cottages in the countryside. I . . . I'm afraid Diarmuid was lost in it."

I blinked, feeling no sense of loss. 'Twas a marvel how drastically my feelings for him had changed, yet Diarmuid was the reason I was here. I rubbed my eyes, wondering if the fire had been the result of my spell. "What of Siobhan?" I asked.

"She died, as did her whole family and Reverend Winthrop, who was celebrating with them. The Highlands have never seen such an act of destruction; 'tis no doubt the fury of the Goddess." Kyra narrowed her eyes, studying me curiously. "So you do not know anything of this?"

"Is that what people think?"

"Some say you cast a spell in your fury over being condemned to die." She nodded toward the guards. "That's why they are so afraid of you today."

I turned toward the guards. One of them caught my eye

and turned away quickly, as if he could avoid a curse by keeping his back turned. And with Reverend Winthrop gone . . . who would see to it that my sentence was carried out? These cowering guards?

The winds of fate had shifted, and I could feel the power of the Goddess swirling around me.

I was not going to die. I knew that now.

"So my spell worked," I said, loud enough for everyone in the square to hear. 'Twas a strange thrill to speak of witch matters before the Christian villagers. Heads snapped toward me in fear, and I smiled. "Yes, the fire was my doing. I used all my powers to punish the evil. They not only persecuted me, they acted on their hatred of my clan every day. They've been persecuting Wodebaynes for years!"

The few people assembled in the square began to disperse in fear. One lady hitched up her skirts and quickly ran off. Two men meandered toward the church as if they were taking an afternoon stroll.

I swung toward the guards, wondering if I would need to shoot dealan-dé to scare them off.

"Don't curse us!" one of them said, covering his face with his hands. "We mean you no harm!"

"I thought you were about to hang me?" I asked.

The heavyset guard shook his head. "We'll not lay a finger on you, as long as you promise not to practice your sorcery on us."

"All right, then . . ." I cast them a fierce look. "Begone, before I turn you into toads or peahens."

They hurried off, not even looking back. I crossed my arms over my belly, aware of the tingling power inside me. My spell had worked. I knew I should feel jubilant—elated! Instead I felt only a compulsion to leave the scene of my trial.

"By the Goddess, I cannot believe I am walking away from my own execution," I said as Kyra and I strode through the town. I was beyond feeling relief as I walked stiffly down the lane.

"So you really did cast a spell?" she asked wonderingly.

"Indeed, and by the grace of the Goddess, she fulfilled it."

"Many say it wasn't the Goddess," she said quietly. "Some say it was dark magick. A huge taibhs."

I sighed. "Let their tongues wag. The spell I cast was just a return of all the evil Siobhan had sent my way, threefold."

Kyra nodded, but I could tell she wasn't convinced. Let her be, I thought. She had always been näive. Someday she would understand.

As I walked home, I was surprised at the respect paid me by passersby. A man with a cart offered me a ride, and two passing ladies actually bowed before me. I knew they had heard of the fires, which had quickly turned me into a local legend, it seemed. I had always known of my powers, but for once it was nice to have others acknowledge my gifts.

When I reached the cottage, I found Síle sitting at the table, staring off at nothingness.

"Are you all right, Ma?"

She looked up at me, startled, as though she were seeing a ghost. Slowly she shook her head, pointing a finger at me. "My fury and disappointment know no bounds. Have you any idea what you have unleashed?"

" 'Twas a spell," I said simply. "A spell against my persecutors—those who would have taken the life of my baby!"

"No evil action deserves the black magick you conjured. I

have never seen anything like it—never! You have caused a split in our coven, some arguing that you created the spell in your own defense. But they are wrong." My ma tried to sniff back tears. "You have created a horrible evil, Rose. Your spell ushers in the advent of a very dark time. A terrible reign of darkness! I have seen it!" Her voice broke in a sob, and she rested her head in her hands, shaking.

I folded my arms, unable to comfort her. "You make it sound as if I were a selfish child. I did not create the spell just for myself. I was acting for all Wodebaynes. This is the type of vengeance our clan needs."

Ma shook her head. "No, Rose. There is nothing anyone could have done to warrant this horrible violence. You didn't only hurt Siobhan—you destroyed her entire family! Her entire coven! And all of the villagers of Lillipool—Vykrothes, Leapvaughns, and Christians alike. You burned little children and women expecting bairns, like yourself."

"I didn't . . . I didn't mean for *that* to happen, but—"

"Oh, dear Goddess!" Síle wailed. "How could my daughter, my own flesh and blood, be capable of such evil?"

I sat down on my bed in disbelief. She didn't understand, and I didn't have the strength to enlighten her. I did not enjoy seeing her in pain like this, though I truly thought she was being overly dramatic.

"It must be Gowan's blood," she muttered. "Your actions make it clear. The evil must have started with him, dabbling in dark magick like a foolish child who knows no better. The man always did want to take the easy road. He must have planted the seed of evil, and now you've nurtured it." She took a deep breath and collapsed into sobs once again.

" 'Tis not so," I said, touching her shoulder. "In time you will understand—"

"I will not!" Ma winced, pulling away from me. "Time will not heal this wound, Rose, and you may not remain under this roof for even a single night." She steeled herself, fixing me with a scowl. "You are not my daughter anymore. I do not care where you go, but I never want to see you again."

Beneath my overriding numbness, I felt the last vestige of hope crushed within me. My mother was abandoning me. My baby and I would have no one in the world, no safe harbor. Only one another.

My mouth felt dry as I moved about the cottage, gathering up my meager belongings. How would it feel never to return here? To have no one to watch over me, to console me over night visions? No one to see that I got enough to eat or had a place to sleep? No one to teach me new spells? No one to help me care for the coming child? Fear tightened my chest at the prospect of walking out the door . . . fear and dread. My mother was the last vestige of my old life, and I longed to cling to her.

But I had no choice. Ma would not have me. She watched me pack like a hawk waiting to pounce.

When I had everything in a satchel, I turned to her. "I'll say good-bye," I told her, "but surely we will meet again?"

She turned her head away and staved me off with one hand. "I cannot bear to lay eyes upon you," she said. "Just begone!"

Swallowing the lump that had formed in my throat, I stepped out the door and ventured into the woods. I had nowhere to go but my sacred circle, and even that seemed tainted by the hands of Diarmuid. Still, I swept the circle and raised my hands to the Goddess.

"I have a need that must be met," I said. "I beg You, Goddess, that I obtain a home, a place to live for me and my babe to come." I stood there under the hazy sky, wondering where I would go. "Goddess, I know You do not intend for me and my child to starve."

I thought of my mother, cursing her weakness. "She has never understood my powers, Goddess." I had always believed that someday I would inherit Ma's stature as high priestess of our coven . . . but now it was not to be. "Perhaps it is envy," I said aloud.

But there was no one to answer. Letting my hands drop to my sides, I realized that this circle had truly lost its magic for me. I packed my tools in my satchel, then set fire to my broom. I swept the wide circle with the flaming broom, wiping it all away. The Goddess would no longer visit this part of the woods. The magick was now gone from the stone altar, the green moss, and the tree that had once served as a Beltane maypole.

Once the circle was broken, I took my satchel and walked down the road. I decided to walk to Lillipool to witness the harvest of my spell. I walked as if in a daze until I reached a section of the woods that was now charred black and nearly empty, as if the trees and cottage there had simply melted into the earth.

I paused, pinching my nose against the smoking ash. What had stood here? I could not remember. I pressed closer, realizing that the striated rows of ash were charred skeletons. Three skeletons pressed against a door. Had they been unable to escape in time? I pressed my hands to my mouth, horrified at the thought. To imagine a sudden fire, the choking smoke, the need to get out before the flames swept over you . . .

Closing my eyes, I swallowed hard, trying to ignore the sting in my throat. 'Twas destruction at the hands of the Goddess, I told myself, and she smites evil. These villagers may have been nothing to me, but surely they were evil?

I didn't feel ready to see more, yet I felt compelled to walk on, past yet another and another scene of the fire, now merely a blackened square upon the earth. When I reached the river, I had a vague sense that the mill had once stood here, with cottages all around. But now I stood amidst a smoky landscape of embers, an endless horizon of ash and blackened earth.

"So mote it be," I said aloud to ward off any doubts I had over the devastation surrounding me.

Down the lane of ashes I saw the charred skeletons of three children lined up, as if prepared for burial rites. I thought of the children I'd seen playing in the dusty square when I'd come to Lillipool to see Diarmuid. A pang of regret tightened in my breast, but again I told myself 'twas the Goddess's will. Were not these children being groomed in the bigoted ways of their clans?

I moved toward the center of what was once Lillipool. The charred skin of a man's hand reached out from a fallen window ledge, though there was no body to be seen. Stepping around it, I shuddered and rubbed my belly. "'Tis a gruesome sight," I said aloud. "But surely he was an evildoer."

Even the dusty village square had been transformed to thick, dark ash. Ashes of bones and buildings, embers of my enemies' dreams and hatred.

So much hatred.

Yet I could feel neither jubilation over the success of my spell nor sorrow for the lives lost upon this doomed patch of the Highlands. The Goddess had pushed me beyond feeling, beyond tears.

Walk. Breathe. Rest. My strength was focused on the simplest matters right now, the need to survive and care for my baby. *See here the fruits of your spell,* the Goddess was telling me. *Witness and learn, for the destruction wrought here is the result of your summons.*

Near the river sat a row of buildings that had not completely burned, but only collapsed into ash. Mayhap the people in them had used the water of the river to fend off the fire? I stepped near one sagging doorway and peered inside. The bodies here were not completely charred, and perhaps they were worse for their rotting stench, their distinguishable features. Was that the tinker? And the children . . .

I turned away, wanting only to see the corpses of those most deserving.

I walked into a tangle of smoking embers that I thought to be Diarmuid's cottage. Kicking at a gray ashen stump, I thought of the hungry look in Diarmuid's eyes the night before. His denial of our love, his retreat from the Goddess's plan. Goddess, please grant me that my child will not have those eyes, those lustful, glittery eyes. . . .

The ash below my shoe crunched apart, lowering me into a burning ember. I stomped out the heat, then noticed two skeletons, their charred limbs entwined.

Could it be Diarmuid and . . . and Siobhan?

Was this the spot where they had died?

I climbed over the ashes to study the skeletons. A gold ring was still wrapped around one of the charred finger bones—Diarmuid's ring. I pressed my lips together, feeling a sting as I understood that the burnt girl was Siobhan.

'Twould be the last time she hurt me.

I reached down and snapped the ring off Diarmuid's charred finger bone. I would save it for my child. "I won't tell your daughter the truth about you," I told him, then thought better of it. How many years had I tried to pry the truth about Da from Ma? "Or mayhap I'll tell her everything . . . every sordid detail of your weak and cowardly character."

I laughed, realizing that Diarmuid no longer had any power in this life. Lifting my gown, I gazed upon the marking that I had branded on my belly. The pentagram was there, inverted. I blinked in awe. I had branded it so that I could look down and see it—but that meant the star shape was actually upside down upon my belly. An inverted pentagram was a legendary symbol for the harnessing of evil, though I'd never known anyone who'd used it.

I pressed Diarmuid's ring against my own inverted marking. Somehow it brought me a dark pleasure, and I was glad to feel something even if it was a bitter end.

"'Tis your heritage," I told my child. "The inverted pentagram, the dark spell, the dark wave, the origin of our redemption. This will be the spell I pass on to you to protect you and yours for all time."

The babe gave a hearty kick, and I lowered my gown. 'Twas time to rest, but I could not find comfort here in this landscape of charred ruin. I tucked the ring into a satchel on my belt and moved on.

Instead of heading back to my own village, I kept going east, past the burnt bog and heather that had surrounded Siobhan's house. I paid no homage to the smoking remains there as I walked past, my sights set on a distant village where I might find lodging at an inn.

I came to a fork in the road and decided to continue east, to the place where the sun rose. Just beyond the fork someone called my name. I turned to find Aislinn waving at me, her red hair flying as she ran to catch up with me. Her energy seemed jarring in the silent woods, the site of so much recent destruction.

"Rose! Rose! It *was* you, wasn't it? Did you see the ruin?" Her face was lit with a predatory smile. "Your spell wiped them out, the whole lot of them! By the Goddess, we really showed them! It will be a long time before anyone else crosses a Wodebayne."

I rocked back on my heels, weary but relieved that Aislinn understood.

"You must be filled with wonder at what you've accomplished."

"I can't say that I am," I admitted, wishing that I could summon some emotion.

"Well, then I am proud on your behalf," Aislinn said. "Your dark wave of a spell has put an end to our persecution. You have altered our fate, Rose. Nevermore will we be downtrodden, nevermore the outcasts."

"My ma does not agree," I said. "She's banished me from our coven."

"Síle is a foolish woman," Aislinn said. "She has no vision, no courage. Did you know that many of us had already abandoned her coven, long before last night? Coveners were tiring of Síle's failure to take action. We've begun to have our own circle in the woods east of here, near a village called Druinden. Though sometimes we flounder. We haven't really found a high priestess with the power to summon the Goddess."

"Really?" I felt bolstered by this news. Perhaps I had not been abandoned as I'd thought. Perhaps it was Síle who was wrong. Perhaps she had been denying the ways of the Goddess, and that was why I was here traveling down this unknown road with barely a stitch to my name.

"Is that where you're headed?" Aislinn asked. "Druinden?"

"I suppose, if I can get a room at the inn there." I felt awkward revealing myself to Aislinn, yet I suspected she knew my entire story already. "I've not only been banished from the coven, but also from the cottage. And . . . you probably know, I'm with child."

"Don't even think of the inn!" she insisted, her face flushing with pride. "You must stay with my sister and me! It's my father's cottage, but he's off at sea most of the time. And you mustn't worry about the bairn. The Goddess will provide. Especially if you decide you want to be high priestess of the new coven. Of course, the others must agree, but how could they not see your power? The whole village of Druinden knows of the dark wave. I'll wager everyone from here to Londinium knows. That spell has made you the high priestess of the Highlands."

I hardly felt like royalty, shuffling down that long road upon my aching feet. At the moment all I wanted was a place to rest and a pitcher of water to wash the smell of death from me. Wash away the soot, and the grime, and the bitter memory of betrayal.

14.
Samhain

" 'Tis time to leave the light and enter the darkness," I said from the center of the circle. My coveners gathered around me, listening intently as their new high priestess spoke the words of the Samhain rite. "I plunge the blade of my athame deep into the heart of my enemy," I said, lowering my athame into a goblet of wine held by Aislinn.

"Plunge the blade, let evil die," they chanted, circling around me.

I went over to the ceremonial fire and stirred it with a stick until embers flew through the darkness. "I stoke the fires of vengeance and point the wrath of the Goddess toward their evil."

"Stoke the fires, let evil die," they chanted.

I stood naked before them, the round ripeness of my body so befitting the harvest ritual. The coveners were also unclad, and I noticed that a few others had taken to branding their bellies with the inverted pentagram. Aislinn had done it first, inspired by the marking on my belly, which had healed but was now a deep brown—a permanent sign of the powerful spell I had created.

Around my neck I wore a necklace with the amber stone Kyra had charged for me along with jet black beads to signify my position as high priestess. I had not seen Kyra or my mother since the day after the dark wave. At times tales of Síle's coven trickled into our circle, and I listened with interest, despite the fact that I knew I would never see my mother again. I realized now how she had tried to undermine my strength, depriving me of the power the Goddess intended me to wield.

I touched the golden stone at my neck, wondering if Kyra knew the power of her charm. Amber was also an excellent protector of children and a spell strengthener, and I often held the charmed stone close to my breast in anticipation of the birthing rite. My child would be here before Imbolc, I knew it. I had enjoyed visions of her—a tiny bundle in my arms as I knelt before Aislinn, summoning the Goddess's power through the lighting of the candles in the crown upon my head.

"Let us reenact the great event of our year," I said, moving to the side of the circle, "the dark wave."

Aislinn led the dance, playing me as I crafted the spell in my prison cell. Other coveners played the forces of earth, wind, water, and fire. As I watched the dancers move, leaping in the air and dipping to the ground, I thought of the hours I had spent schooling my coveners in the elements of the dark wave. We planned to cast the spell over the Burnhydes to the north, for they had been stealing sheep from Wodebayne herders repeatedly. 'Twas unforgivable, the way they committed crime with abandon. "They must be stopped," Aislinn said often. "And we have the power to do it."

The dark wave.

The coveners had proven to be apt students of the grave spell. Already they had collected hair and fingernails from Burnhydes for use in the magick.

My baby shifted inside me, and I smiled. Aye, little one, you will learn the spell, too. I will pass it on to you. It is your legacy.

When the drama before me ended, I arose and held my hands up to the Goddess. "I fell into deep darkness," I said. "I greeted death. I tore the velvet darkness of everlasting light. Ablaze with glory, I was reborn. Now the old year ends."

"The new year begins!" the coveners responded. "Plunge the blade! Stoke the fires!"

I went to the center of the circle, saying: "Their evil shall burn their own funeral pyres!"

The coveners danced around me, chanting: "Plunge the blade! Stoke the fires!"

I felt the power of the Goddess swirl around us. Aye, we were nearly ready to send the dark wave, so mote it be. "Welcome, new year, farewell, strife. From fiery embers arises life."

"Plunge the blade! Stoke the fires. . . ."

Epilogue

Hunter and I still sat silently on the couch. *Plunge the blade! Stoke the fires!* The words kept running through my head, like a mantra. This girl, this young, seventeen-year-old girl. I tried to imagine going through what she went through. Would I have reacted the same way?

"Morgan?"

I realized that Hunter was looking at me with concern. His hand lay on my arm. He seemed to be waiting for me to respond. Had he asked me a question? I shook my head, trying to clear it, and then reached for my cold chamomile tea. "Yes," I said quietly. When I raised the cup to my lips, I realized that my face was wet with tears.

"Morgan, are you all right?"

I looked down at the closed book. Rose MacEwan, I thought, my ancestor. The creator of the dark wave. How was it possible? But I knew, I realized almost immediately, with a sinking feeling in the pit of my stomach. I remembered the few times I had practiced dark magick—shape-shifting with Ciaran. Weather magick with my half brother Killian. It had felt so right, pure, and natural. Hunter realized it, too, I thought—when strange things had started happening at our circles, he had believed it was me. Rose could have been me, I thought with sickening clarity. We were so alike: blood relatives. *I could have been Rose.*

Hunter had knelt on the floor before me, and he sat now with his hands on my knees, begging me to speak.

"No," I said softly, shaking my head. "I don't know what I am."

Hunter looked up at me, his eyes warm with concern. I could see pain there, pain at seeing me cry. Oh, Goddess, he loved me, without tricks or reservations. What he had done with Justine seemed so trivial now.

He sat back on the couch, reached out, and folded me into his arms. I didn't resist. "She didn't know, love. She didn't know what she was doing."

"But she still did it." I shivered involuntarily, thinking of Rose and Diarmuid—she had been so sure of their love, as sure as I had been—*was*—of Hunter's. And look where it had led. The same place my birth parents' love had led—to death, destruction, and misery.

I looked up at Hunter's face—the face that I dreamed of, the face that I believed to be there for me. Only me. I reached up and touched Hunter's cheek—my mùirn beatha dàn. Even his parents' love had led to hurt—abandoning their children, Hunter's father hurting himself in an attempt to re-create what they had had after his love's death.

"I know you, love. You're not like Rose. You've chosen good." Hunter whispered, stroking my hair.

I nodded, wanting to believe him. But as a daughter of such dark origins, I could only hope that he was right.